Sapphire Waves

KRISTY MCCAFFREY

SAPPHIRE WAVES

THE PATHWAY SERIES BOOK 7

KRISTY MCCAFFREY

A PATHWAY NOVELLA

The Pathway Series

Deep Blue
Cold Horizon
Ancient Winds
Sapphire Waves

Blue Sage (related novella)

Deep Blue Australia*
Deep Blue Réunion Island*
Deep Blue Cocos Island*
Deep Blue Hawai'i*
Cold Horizon Telluride*
Shark Reef*

*Short stories in the Pathway universe

Sapphire Waves

Cover Design: Okay Creations - okaycreations.com

Illustrator: Penny Fournier - instagram.com/penny.illustration

Editor: Mimi The Grammar Chick – merrelli.wixsite.com/grammarchick

Proofreader: Julie Evans

Author Photo: Katy McCaffrey – instagram.com/katymccaffreyphoto

E-book ISBN-13: 978-1-9528013-7-2

Print ISBN-13: 978-1-9528013-8-9

kmccaffrey.com

kristy@kmccaffrey.com

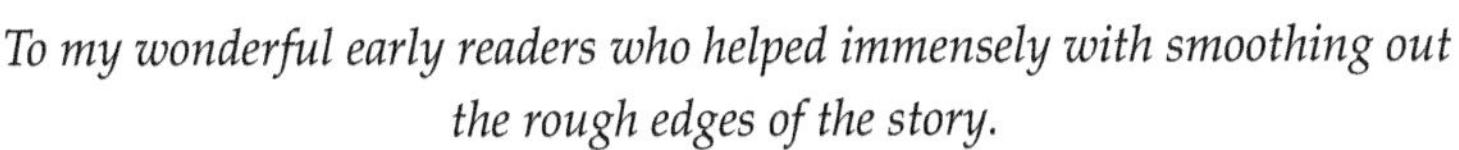

To my wonderful early readers who helped immensely with smoothing out the rough edges of the story.

To my editor and proofreader for the final polish.

And to my husband - my best plotting partner.

CHAPTER 1

The Bahamas
Abaco Island
Early December

Missy hoisted her pack, grabbed her large duffel bag filled with scuba gear and personal items, and headed toward the large white van waiting in front of her hotel.

"Missy?" Dr. Ken Mansfield greeted her with a smile. He'd aged since she'd last seen him several years ago, but he still had that weather-worn, tanned appearance, although his hair had gone whiter.

She shook his hand with her lone free one. "Ken, it's good to see you."

"I'm glad that Sarah was able to bring you on board."

"Happy to help."

Ken worked at the Mote Marine Laboratory and Aquarium at Georgia Tech as well as consulting with NOAA on their Ocean Exploration and Research projects. He was the leader of this expedition to a blue hole located off the coast of Abaco. His associate, Sarah Fischer, had invited Missy when their safety diver had fallen through at the last minute.

According to Sarah, the goal of the project was to map the hole and gather water samples and sediment cores for further analysis in a lab. Missy's job was to keep an eye on the crew while in the water.

"How was your flight?" Ken asked. "You came from San Francisco?"

"Yes. And it was good."

"Ready to go diving?"

"Absolutely. Am I the first pickup?"

"Yep. Climb aboard."

The driver stashed her gear in the back, and Missy settled onto the first bench seat, her sturdy traveling purse crosswise across her body. She wore capris and lightweight slip-on sneakers and a breezy blouse. She was in the Bahamas, after all. While it would be for work, she was going to enjoy a bit of down time as well.

Her last major expedition over a year ago had been much different than the one she was about to embark on. She'd accompanied her best friend, Dr. Grace Mann, on a three-week trip to Guadalupe Island in Baja, California. Mostly, Missy had gone to offer moral support and for the adventure—Grace not only had been testing a prototype of her shark detection array, she also had been filmed for a documentary. But those two goals aside, Grace's main focus had been to free dive with the abundant population of great white sharks that congregated each fall, and Missy had joined her, believing she could handle swimming with some of the largest water predators on earth.

Turned out, she couldn't.

She simply didn't have the undying love that Gracie had for the fish. Missy also couldn't separate her need to stay alive and her resolve to complete the dives. Somehow, Grace could control her fear in such situations, but Missy had found it exceedingly difficult.

Determined to get past the anxiety the expedition had introduced into her life, Missy had decided to pursue a long dormant dream—to become a tech diver. And for the last year, she'd been working hard at it. When Sarah had called with her offer to join their team, Missy couldn't have been happier. It was exactly what she'd been training for, and she'd said yes before knowing all the details, because for once in her life the details didn't matter.

Unbidden, Josh McKittrick flashed into her mind. She hadn't been to the Bahamas since her brief time at the Shark Lab on Bimini. Four years ago. Four years since she'd last seen him.

What was he up to? Not that she had any right to know. She'd cut him loose during the most difficult period of her life. At the time, it had seemed the right thing to do.

But, damn, the regret still managed to strike red-hot at times, and its recurrence annoyed her. She should be over this. She *was* over this.

Ken jumped into the front passenger seat, and the driver soon had them out on the roadway, heading to the next hotel to pick up team members.

"I guess we all should've stayed at the same property," Missy remarked.

Ken smiled. "Oh, it's all right. Some of the crew came in early to get a little vacation time in. Everyone's needs are different. Some like the big resorts, others like something off the beaten path."

That would've been Josh. Why was she thinking about him so much? It had to be the locale. Although she wasn't on Bimini—it was the westernmost district of the Bahamas—Abaco had the same atmosphere of humid tropics and lazy afternoons spent on the beach.

She'd entertained the idea of making amends with him, but as months had turned to years, she'd convinced herself there was no point. So she quietly and resolutely had buried the sharp longing that managed to survive the forest burn of the memories of that relationship, however brief it had been, and she had allowed herself to stalk him only a few times on social media, which unfortunately had confirmed that he was in a relationship with someone named Tory, and he was living in Houston. After that, she'd forced herself to put him out of her mind.

Besides, if he weren't still with Tory then he most assuredly was married to a gorgeous marine biologist with 2.5 kids. Missy didn't need to torture herself with confirming it either way.

Yet, no matter how much she tried to intellectualize her relationship with McKittrick, and her ending it the only way that had made sense back then, her heart managed to still whisper to her, *You let him get away. You were so fucking stupid.*

She had to concede that she had been. Maybe not stupid, just not aware enough to understand what Josh had meant to her.

They turned right and stopped at the entrance of another hotel where two people waited. Missy didn't know either of them. She didn't think she would know any of the additional team members, save Sarah.

The new arrivals were soon settled in the seat behind her, introduced as Andy Riley, geologist, and Lucy Eastman, microbiologist. They appeared to be friends. Polite introductions were exchanged, with Andy and Lucy giving her a slightly confused look when she told them she studied cephalopods.

"Are we expecting some extraordinary octopi in the hole?" Andy asked, his dark bushy eyebrows crashing together and forming a definite unibrow.

"No," Missy said with a laugh. "I'm here to function as the safety diver. But who knows? Maybe we'll find something new down there."

"I'm counting on it," Lucy replied, a thick brown braid draped across her shoulder. "Lots of microbes, I'm thinking. Maybe even something that was around during the formation of the Earth."

"Really?" Missy asked. "Are we talking billions of years?"

Lucy nodded. "I'd say so."

Missy went back to watching the scenery as Andy and Lucy started chatting.

The next stop produced Dr. Sarah Fischer, who greeted Missy warmly with a hug. "I'm so glad you've joined us," Sarah said, her blonde hair pulled back in a ponytail, her strong German features dotted with freckles and a slight sunburn.

"Me too," Missy replied, and meant it. Anticipation for the next two weeks filled her. She genuinely liked Sarah and Ken, and Lucy and Andy seemed friendly enough, so the team dynamics were shaping up to be good, always a plus.

The next hotel was only a few minutes away. Missy and Sarah had started discussing some of the details of the blue hole when the van rounded a driveway, and Missy lost the thread of the conversation. Her heartrate accelerated from zero to sixty with lightning speed. The man waiting in front of the hotel wore a ballcap and was slim and fit in a navy-blue t-shirt and khaki shorts. A pack was slung over one shoulder and mirrored sunglasses hid his eyes, but she would know him anywhere ….

"That's Josh McKittrick," Sarah said when she caught sight of him. "Do you know him?"

Missy cleared her throat, willing her racing heart to calm down. "Yes," she uttered.

"He's the one in charge of our benthic lander," Sarah added.

The van pulled to a stop and Sarah hopped out. She shook Josh's hand and started chatting with him.

Missy was still grappling with her shock. Is this why she'd been thinking about him? Because the universe was about to play a wicked trick on her?

Four years ago, Josh had been flash fire in her veins, and it had honestly scared her. And then her dad had suffered a heart attack. Missy had been unable to handle much past that, least of all an intense relationship that was threatening to consume her. She'd done the only thing she could—she went home to California, tearfully said goodbye to her father within twenty minutes of arriving at the hospital, and then a few days later broke up with Josh over the phone.

She remained rooted in her seat, sweat breaking out on every inch of her. It wasn't that she'd never envisioned seeing him again—they both worked in marine science, so it was bound to happen at some point—but she really thought she'd be able to handle it better.

He still looked the same, if a bit more filled out with broader shoulders and forearms that hinted at muscles further up. Dark brown hair peeked out from beneath his hat, and Missy remembered running her fingers through the sweaty locks when they would sneak off to a remote beach on Bimini and ….

He removed his glasses and even from here she could see his blue eyes. They had always been his best feature. Well, that and his hands.

Oh Lord. She nervously tugged at the messy bun she'd thrown her hair into this morning and looked anywhere but at him talking to Sarah. She didn't want to seem obvious.

"Missy?"

His deep voice shot straight through her, reminding her of the time she'd been zapped by an electric eel. She raised her gaze to his.

"Hi, Josh. Good to see you again." She was glad her voice sounded normal, because she sure as hell didn't feel normal.

His eyes, still so familiar to her that her stomach clenched from the grief of missing him all this time, turned dark and swirled with confusion. Or maybe it was animosity. Missy couldn't be certain.

"I didn't know you were going to be here," he said, his tone flat, but Missy was sure she heard panic buried somewhere in there.

Shit. This was a disaster. She quelled the urge to bolt from the van and run.

I'm an adult. I can deal with this.

She'd made a commitment to Sarah and the team, and Missy prided herself on her work ethic. Just another small thing of Josh's that had rubbed off on her during their stint on Bimini.

She shrugged and gave a look of *well-here-I-am*.

The driver stashed the last of the gear, so Sarah said, "How great you two know each other. Why don't you sit together? I'll go to the back."

Missy remained silent while everyone took their seats, Josh folding his large frame beside hers, tucking his backpack at his feet, which were covered in old ratty tennis shoes.

"I see some things never change," she said, glancing down at his footwear, starting to feel a bit calmer. The worst was over, she told herself.

"I suppose they don't. You look great, Rembert." He sounded sincere and a bit pained as he looked away.

Missy basked in the compliment while at the same time feeling like she'd done something wrong. The urge to reach out and grip his hand hit her. She turned away as well to get her emotions under control, mindlessly watching palm trees pass by as the van raced down a winding two-lane road.

Her relationship with Josh had been a hot and lusty thing, but it had lasted only three weeks. Maybe four? And he'd certainly not argued with her when she'd ended it, so it had obviously not meant much to him. He was surely far over it by now.

But she had a chance to make amends, to perhaps restore a bit of the friendship they had enjoyed in the beginning.

Hell, who was she kidding? Josh hadn't exactly been the friendly type back then. They had gone straight from acquaintances to lovers. There'd been no friendship in between. Maybe that had been their problem.

No. The problem had been her. When she'd lost her dad, she'd cleared everything from her life that took too much energy. And Josh had been at the top of that list.

"What are you up to these days?" she asked. *And where is Tory what's-her-name?*

"I've been working at Undersea Solution Labs for the past three years."

"That's in Houston, right?" she asked, pretending not to know. But the next question was genuine. "How do you do marine science while being landlocked?"

"Well, Houston isn't far from Galveston if we need to go in-water, but I'm mostly on the engineering side."

"Still working on the Bat Suit?" she asked, referring to the swimming apparatus he'd been designing when they'd been at Bimini together.

"Kinda moved on from that. My new toy is called Benji."

"Oh," Missy said, suddenly realizing the connection. "You've designed the benthic lander."

"Yep, it's my baby."

"Is this the first time you're deploying it?"

He nodded. "We did preliminary tests in Galveston, but this will be the first blue hole, so the conditions will be trickier. How about you?"

"I switched from sharks to cephalopods. I work as a postdoctoral fellow at the Brown Aquarium Research Institute."

"BARI?"

She nodded.

"That's impressive," he said. "I've tried applying there myself."

How close had they come to working with one another?

"I'm glad you were able to stay near your mom," he added. "I know it was hard when you lost your dad."

Missy's throat tightened. It was still a bit raw, even after all this time. Or maybe it was because it had happened when she'd been at Bimini. With Josh.

"Yeah, it was good that I could stay close," she said. *And end things with you.* It hung in the air as if Missy had said it aloud.

The two things in her life that had been inexorably linked.

While seeing Josh was better than she'd hoped, it also brought with it the pain of that time. She really wasn't of a mind to go there. Not now.

"Are you married?" she blurted out. So much for playing it cool.

"No. You?"

She shook her head.

"I guess I should take comfort in that," he said.

Still tongue-tied from her obvious interest in his love life, all she could do was give him her best quizzical look.

"You're not the marrying type," he added.

"What's that supposed to mean?" she asked, chagrined, keeping her voice low since she had no desire to let everyone in the van know about her history with Josh.

He gave her his full attention. "I'd thought it was me, but maybe I've been wrong all this time. It was you."

She wasn't just tongue-tied—her throat felt full of cotton.

Ken turned from his position in the front passenger seat and said something to Josh, effectively ending her showdown with her ex, which was just as well.

Missy was rattled.

Because he was right.

It had been her. All her.

And she had nothing but the bitter taste of regret in her mouth.

CHAPTER 2

Bimini Shark Lab
January
Four years earlier …

Missy dropped her duffel in the cabin she'd been assigned at the Bimini Biological Field Station, a small room with two sets of bunk beds and a desk clearly meant to be shared.

Excitement coursed through her. Getting accepted into the shark program was a real coup, and it didn't hurt that Shark Lab was on South Bimini, part of several islands in the Bimini chain, considered by many, her fisherman father included, to be the fishing capital of the world. She'd been here once or twice as a girl, but her memories had been those of a child; now she looked forward to sharing her adventures as an adult with her dad when this was all over. In the meantime, she'd be spending the next three months on an island in the Bahamas. Not a bad gig.

A girl with blonde hair entered the room. "Hi," she said. "Are you new?"

"Yes. Missy Rembert."

"Grace Mann," she replied, shaking Missy's hand. "Nice to meet you. Both top bunks are free."

"Thanks."

"You can store your stuff here." Grace indicated the space beneath one of the bottom bunks. "Only one desk, so grab an empty piece of real estate on it to stack your stuff. There's only three of us in here." She pointed at the lower bunk against the far wall. "That's Jen Fairfield, but she's not here right now. Where are you from?"

"San Francisco."

"Sweet. I grew up in Orinda."

"We're practically neighbors," Missy said, liking Grace immediately.

"What's your area of study?"

"I'm looking at whether all sharks are apex predators on reefs, or just some."

"I like it."

"And you?" Missy asked.

Grace's face lit up. "I'm trying to build a sonar array to identify shark species in the open ocean. I'm experimenting with the lemon sharks here, mostly the youngsters that hang out in the mangroves."

"That sounds ambitious. If I'm able, I'd love to help, but you probably have a line of people."

Grace laughed. "No, you're the first. You hungry?"

"Sure."

Grace waved her forward. "Follow me to the mess hall. We can grab lunch before the bulk of the other interns return from checking the long lines."

Missy followed Grace down a hallway that ended in a kitchen. A woman had prepared turkey sandwiches and they each took a plate with potato chips and a can of soda, and then took a seat in faded plastic chairs around one of four tables.

As they chatted, Missy learned that Grace's dad had been none other than Dr. Eddie Mann, a well-known biologist who had studied great whites for years before his death. It almost made Missy a little starry-eyed, feeling as if she were in the company of ocean royalty. However, she soon relaxed when it became apparent that Grace was down-to-earth except for an obsession with her work, which included being a computer nerd.

With lunch nearing its conclusion, a commotion outside caught their attention.

"What's going on?" Missy asked.

Grace huffed. "Josh McKittrick." She stood and deposited her plate in a nearby bin, then headed to the door. Missy quickly followed suit.

Once outside, they encountered a truck pulling a trailer and several men, most looking like locals, trying to hoist something off, hence all the yelling. One man, taller than the others and wearing the rattiest tennis shoes she'd ever seen, appeared to be in charge, barking orders as they lifted a large, elongated cage and deposited it on a wooden platform near the building.

"What is that?" Missy asked, shielding her eyes from the late afternoon sun.

Grace's face pinched in consternation. "I'm not sure. I haven't seen this one yet. Josh is here like the rest of us doing an internship, but he's more interested in the mechanical stuff."

"Like your sonar array?"

"Hmm." Grace considered the parallel. "A little. But the crux of mine will be in the computer programming. A deep learning algorithm. Josh is all about the parts. I've got some paperwork I have to catch up on, so I'll see you later?"

"Sounds good," Missy replied. "Thanks for the welcome."

"Well, there's a lot of testosterone around here. We girls have to stick together." With a wave, Grace returned to the door they'd just exited. Shark Lab was several buildings that had been linked into one huge building. Missy had heard that at one time it was a police barracks before the lab was established by Samuel "Doc" Gruber.

Missy glanced at her watch. She was supposed to meet with a woman named Ruth, the station manager, around three p.m. to get oriented. Since she still had an hour, she stayed on the porch to watch the show.

The locals all piled back into the truck and left, leaving her alone with McKittrick and his contraption. He was trying to loosen something when he started swearing.

Suddenly feeling funny about standing around and gawking at the man, Missy turned toward the lab when McKittrick's voice stopped her.

"Hey. Could you give me a hand?"

She glanced back. "Sure." She came down the few steps and went to his side.

He lifted his gaze. "Are you new?" he asked.

She stopped short, speechless. His eyes were so blue. From the porch she hadn't been able to see them, but up close ....

She cleared her throat. "Yes. Just arrived. I'm Missy Rembert."

With one hand still in the contraption, he lifted his other to greet her, extending his palm. "I'm Josh."

They shook hands, and she tried to ignore the frisson of energy the action left in its wake. Josh was cute, to be certain, but she was determined not to be led astray by muscles and hormones. Shark Lab was a difficult internship to garner. She didn't want to waste the opportunity by going boy crazy.

"Nice to meet you," she said.

"I need you to stick your fingers in here and hold this lever down." He took the hand he'd just held and guided it into position.

She couldn't help but feel that the only reason he'd introduced himself with a handshake was to determine if her digits would help him with this task. Apparently, she'd passed his test.

She did as he asked and a latch released, allowing a door to swing upward so someone could enter the cage.

"What is this?" she asked.

"A self-propelled ocean cage."

She noticed the engine anchored to the back. "You're gonna dive in this thing?"

"That's the plan."

"Is there a purpose to it?"

"Since we're at Shark Lab, I'll give you one guess."

Ignoring the subtle jab, she said, "You're gonna chase sharks."

A large black and white dog came tearing around the corner of the lab building, causing Missy to jump. She backed up until she bumped into Josh, who chuckled, his breath warm on the nape of her neck.

"Samson, stay," Josh's said, his voice firm in her ear.

The dog skidded to a halt, tail wagging and tongue hanging out. He was a fit and muscular American bulldog.

"Is he friendly?" Missy asked.

"To a fault."

Josh stepped away, making her realize he'd remained near her for longer than was polite. But he probably thought she was afraid of dogs and was just trying to help.

Another dog bounded forward, a black colored mutt, breaking the concentration of Samson, and the two of them wrestled for a moment before flying forward into Missy.

She laughed, determined to show McKittrick that she was, in fact, a dog lover. Why this was so important to her, she had no idea.

"Hello, sweet boys," she crooned as she leaned over, and they attacked her face with sloppy kisses.

"The other one is a she," Josh said. "Her name is Delilah. They live here at the lab, but be careful, Samson is Vice President. He can get you booted out of the program if he doesn't like you."

"Is that so?" But her question was for the dog and not Josh. "Well Samson and Delilah, if you live up to your namesakes then I guess you're both in for a big tragic love affair."

"It's only tragic if one of them has a bone and the other doesn't. Would you mind taking them inside?"

"No problem. C'mon, guys." She patted her leg and started toward the door. Luckily the mutts were still enamored of her and followed.

"Hey, Missy."

She turned back.

"Welcome to Bimini."

She smiled. "Thanks."

CHAPTER 3

Present Day

Josh reached into his pack and pulled out a packet of gummy bears.

"You still eating those things?" Missy asked.

He nodded, tearing the bag open and popping one into his mouth. It was his stress food, and if ever there was a stressful situation, this was it.

Missy Rembert. He'd come to accept that he'd likely never see her again. And now that he had, he was beginning to wish he hadn't. He didn't appreciate the tightness in his chest or the constriction of his throat as he sat beside her, pretending that she hadn't completely broken his heart almost four years ago.

He was over her. He really was.

"I'm guessing you're still in touch with Grace," he said, dumping a handful of the chewy candy into his palm and then dropping all of them into his mouth. Apparently, one wasn't enough.

"Yes. She lives in Monterey, and I see her often. Maybe you caught her documentary that came out earlier this year?"

He'd heard about it, but he'd learned through mutual channels that Missy had been with Grace on that expedition, and he didn't really need to watch something that would throw him into a funk, so he'd skipped it.

"I'm afraid I missed it," he said. "How was it?"

"Fantastic," she said with a laugh. "I was there, and I briefly got in the water with her, but coming face to face with some of the biggest great whites on earth quickly killed my brave factor, and I left her to it."

"She was more shark-obsessed than most. I'm not surprised."

"She hasn't changed, but at least she's got herself a boyfriend to keep an eye on her."

"Brad?" That would be a shame since Brad Michaels was an asshat.

"No. She finally wised up and dumped him. She's with Alec Galloway now. He filmed the doc about her. He's a good mensch. You'd like him."

"I'm glad to hear things worked out for her," he said. "Please give her my best the next time you talk to her."

"I will. I still see Jen Fairfield sometimes too. She works with Grace at CMI. She's been studying whites in the Chatham Islands."

"Sounds rough. Seems like everyone stayed with sharks except you." He chanced a glance at her face and for a brief moment was held spellbound by her green eyes, reminding him of the first time they'd met, in front of Shark Lab when he'd asked for her help with his Bat Suit.

He hadn't really needed her assistance, but it had seemed like a good excuse to introduce himself, since Grace had departed before offering. Some of the guys back then had been known to chase the new female arrivals, and it had irritated Grace, hence why she never went out of her way to make introductions. Josh wasn't one of them, and Grace knew it, but she'd clumped him into the group anyway.

But Missy had been different, even at first glance.

Damn. Looking at her now, it was apparent she was still the most beautiful woman he'd ever known.

He glanced away as the van pulled up to the hotel. Everyone piled out and grabbed their bags.

"Get settled in your rooms," Ken said, "then let's meet in the lobby in an hour."

Josh lost Missy in the hustle of getting everyone checked in, but after dropping his bags in his room, he reorganized his gear and grabbed a duffel bag filled with necessities before returning to the lobby. Sarah was talking to Missy.

She looked good—better than good, if he was being honest—still fit and athletic, her cheeks sporting a recent sunburn, her brown hair pulled back into a ponytail. The memories of their nights together, frantic and desperate at times, hot and filled with longing, accosted him. The more time he'd spent with her, the deeper he'd fallen. He hadn't realized just how far until the day she'd left.

Sarah greeted him with a smile. "Hey, Ken needs another hour to get organized, so we'll meet back here at one p.m."

Josh gave a nod, trying to ignore Missy standing beside the woman.

"I'm starved," Missy said. "How about I buy everyone lunch?"

"I'm gonna take a pass," Sarah said. "I want to check my emails, but you two go ahead." She turned and left them alone.

"What do you say, McKittrick? Are you hungry?"

He stopped his mind from going any further with that question and down a path of no return, and he almost said no. There was no reason to pursue any type of friendship with Missy. The moment he'd seen her in the van had solidified that sentiment.

"Sure," he replied. His heart was seriously falling behind his brain. How could he not grab any morsel of time with her, even if it were a casual meal as friends? He could absolutely handle this.

He fell into step beside her, and they walked to the hotel restaurant. They soon were seated at a breezy outdoor table overlooking the ocean. The hostess gave them menus and Missy began perusing hers.

Without looking up, she said, "Still eating fish burgers?"

"Always." A glance at the menu confirmed that his favorite food item was listed. With no need to read further, he set the menu aside, settled back in his cushioned chair, and took in the view. Damn, he was happy to see her.

"How've you been, Rembert?" he asked, his question sincere.

She lifted her gaze, her eyes flashing with confusion and her forehead pinching into a wrinkle of tension. Or maybe he was imagining the whole thing.

"I've been all right," she said. She cleared her throat and was about to continue talking when the waitress interrupted them.

He ordered the fish burger and Missy went for the cheeseburger. She suggested they share an order of French fries, and he silently agreed. Then she asked with a raised eyebrow, "Beer?"

"Why not," he said. This trip was already shaping up to be a lot more than he'd bargained for. He figured he deserved at least one drink stronger than water or cola.

The waitress departed, and an awkward silence descended between them.

"I owe you an apology," she finally said.

He waited. Because she did.

"Back then, I was ...."

"Were you happy?" he asked, and then because he couldn't help himself, he added, "With me?"

"Yes," she answered with no hesitation.

"Then why?"

"Losing my dad threw me off. I didn't want to be close to anyone."

"Even me?"

"Especially you," she replied in a quiet voice.

The waitress returned with two glasses of cold beer, depositing them on the table.

Josh took a big drink, then said, "So you pushed everyone away."

Missy also took a long swig of her drink and muttered, "Pretty much."

"I never pegged you for a coward, Rembert."

"Well," she said with a sardonic laugh, "now you know." She took another drink and then looked him in the eye. "I'm sorry. If I could go back, I'd change how I handled it."

"In what way?" The question was out before he could stop it. He'd moved on. Why was he pushing this?

She paused, clearly considering what to say, then murmured behind her glass, "I guess I wouldn't have been such a coward."

"Bullshit, Missy. You're no coward. You could've called me anytime."

"I did."

His heart sped up. Had she reached out? Had she wanted to patch things up? But then he reined in the hope that was beginning to run rampant. *Don't be a fool again, Josh.* "The breakup?" he asked.

She gave one stiff nod, confirming the reality that was the end of their relationship. She had ended it and hadn't looked back.

"And I figured Tory wouldn't appreciate an old flame checking in," she added.

Wait. "Tory?" he said, but he knew who she meant.

"Your girlfriend."

Missy *had* been keeping track of him over the years. His clenched stomach loosened a bit. While the thought of stringing Missy along with the idea that he was blissfully happy with someone else crossed his mind, he'd never had much patience with playing games.

"She's not my girlfriend," he answered. "She barely was." There'd been a few others, of course, but nothing had lasted. None of them had been Missy.

Their food arrived, and Missy squirted ketchup on the plate that held the fries. "How's your family?" she asked.

"The same. My folks are still based in Phoenix, but I believe they're in Brazil right now on a geology assignment. Chris is in Australia working for a petroleum company." His older brother had followed in the family business and had gone straight into geology like their parents.

"Do you like living in Houston?" she asked.

"It's all right. I wouldn't mind moving." Before she could question him further, he added, "What about you? Sick of San Francisco yet?"

She shrugged. "After my dad died, I took a semester off to stay with my mom, then I went back to USC for my Ph.D. I'd planned to go somewhere else since I'd done my bachelor's and master's degrees there, but I thought I should stay near my mom."

"Is that why you're still in California?" She looked surprised, so he added a bit sheepishly, "You're not the only one who was keeping tabs."

Her brief smile seemed genuine. "Yes," she replied. "I don't live far from Mom. I'd say it's been good for her, but I've needed her just as much."

"Do you like working for BARI?"

She nodded, taking a bite of her cheeseburger. She wiped her mouth with a napkin and said, "They've let me develop their research into various octopus and cuttlefish species. It's been fantastic. I love it."

With his beer glass empty, he switched to water. "I really thought you'd end up in some type of fishery capacity."

"Because of my dad?" She smiled. "Strangely enough, cephalopods make me feel close to him. After he died and I couldn't bring myself to go back to school right away, I volunteered at the Aquarium of the Bay, doing mostly grunt work, and it helped to keep my mind off things."

Like you.

The unspoken words hung in the air as if she'd said them aloud.

"Eventually, they let me take care of the marine invertebrates," she continued. "I fed the animals and maintained their tanks. That's when I befriended one of the North Pacific bigeye octopus that had been collected on a deep-sea trawl. Most of the octopus didn't really like me—they wouldn't let me touch them and would often squirt water at me, but there was one who I called Piper. She'd allow me to pick her up, and she'd wrap her eight arms around my hand and latch onto my fingers with her suckers. She liked being in enclosed spaces, so I would often bring in recycled glass jars and plastic bins for her. Octopus can't hear but they can sense vibrations, so I would always talk to her when I arrived. I think she recognized me because she would wiggle her arms back and forth like she was waving.

"She died, of course, within a few months. If there's one negative about octopus, it's that they have such very short lives. But she rallied far longer than the staff thought she would, and just before she passed, she laid three eggs, which was extraordinary because they weren't viable since she'd been unable to mate. Losing her devastated me, but it seemed par for the course. I'd lost my dad, I'd lost you. Losing her was just one more thing to endure."

"You didn't lose me, Rembert. You pushed me away."

She tossed her napkin on the table, having eaten most of her burger. "I know. But back then, it was just a big jumble of loss, and I didn't much differentiate any of it."

"So you poured all your focus into the octopus."

"Something like that," she said.

"Then what are you doing here?"

"I met Sarah a few years ago at a marine conference and we've stayed in touch. She knew I'd been working on my safety diver certification and invited me. To be honest, it sounded like fun." Then, she added, "I had no idea you'd be here."

He ignored the jab of pain her statement caused. "You're saying if you'd known then you wouldn't have come."

"Probably." She took a drink. "Yes."

"It appears the universe is conspiring against your cowardice."

"You're saying it's fate we've met again?"

"You always believed in that more than I did," he said. "But maybe we can be friends now."

He cringed as he said it, but he was older and more mature now. He didn't want to keep nursing the pain that Missy had inflicted back then. Life was too short. And he'd loved her. Hell, he loved her still. Maybe he should've told her four years ago. Maybe she wouldn't have left.

"Friends?" she said. Ambivalence flashed across her face but then she settled into acceptance. "I'd like that."

His attention was drawn to three men being seated at a table behind Missy. "What the hell?" he muttered.

Missy swiveled in her seat to follow his gaze, her body stiffening, and said, "What is Brad Michaels doing here?"

CHAPTER 4

Four years ago …

Josh was grabbing a stack of mail when Grace Mann intercepted him in the office.

"I heard you're testing your Bat Suit again," she said, using the nickname the other interns had given his streamlined underwater apparatus designed to shadow sharks in real time. He didn't particularly care for the moniker, but no one would use his choice of Shark Chaser, claiming it sounded like something that would come after a shot of tequila, and sharks were never number two.

"Yep."

"Planning on getting lost again?"

He looked at her pointedly. "Do you have a point, Mann?"

He still had some glitches to work out, but the biggest sticking point concerned his location underwater as he was trying to keep pace with a tiger or bull shark. The topside boat had trouble keeping track of him. In the first trial run, he'd been stranded for over an hour when the crew had lost his location.

"Well, besides that you need some sort of GPS transmitter with an accompanying receiver on the boat—"

"I know," he interrupted. Grace could be a bit annoying with her computer science background, and she wasn't telling him anything he hadn't already considered. The problem, however, was funding. In short, he didn't have much.

She narrowed her eyes, her irritation with him apparent. He and Grace had a sibling type of relationship. She and Brad Michaels had arrived from the University of Miami as a couple, and while they kept the relationship fairly quiet, Josh was still baffled as to why she would go for a guy like that. Michaels was on par with dogshit, although that was a disservice to Samson and Delilah. Josh was tempted to play big brother and scare Brad off, but Grace was stubborn, and he was pretty sure she'd be pissed if he interfered.

Grace crossed her arms. "Well, maybe I won't help you then."

"No offense, Grace, but you're not much of a boat captain. I'll pass."

"Good grief, Josh. I'm probably one of the few friends you have left. You keep burning too many bridges."

He frowned. "No, I don't. I just can't tolerate laziness and lack of focus. *You* of all people should appreciate that." Grace's work ethic matched his own. She was one of the few interns around here he respected. "Tell me how you think you can help me."

"The new girl, Missy."

"You setting me up?" He hadn't been distracted by a woman in a long time, but Rembert had an infectious smile that had caught his attention on more than one occasion. All the more reason to avoid her.

Grace tucked her blonde hair behind an ear. "You're joking, right? You know what your nickname is around here."

This was new. "No," he said slowly.

"Monk. As in celibate. You've never hooked up with anyone."

"That you know of," he countered.

She silently watched him, her right eyebrow arching.

"Okay, fine. I didn't come to Shark Lab to get laid."

"Most of the females have noticed. Anyway," she said, waving her hand to move on to another subject, "I think Missy can drive the boat. I think she might be able to track you."

"What makes you say that?"

"Her dad was a fisherman. She spent a lot of time on boats. Look, I think you should give her a chance. And it's not like you have too many other options. Maybe she's been what you're looking for."

Missy's green eyes flashed in his head as well as the curves that had been distracting him. But he reminded himself one more time that her fun-loving personality wasn't his type.

"Yeah, fine," he heard himself say, ignoring the kick of his pulse.

"Great!" Grace smiled. "I'll tell her. When are you going out?"

"This afternoon."

"We'll be there."

"Hey," he said. "In case you're planning on inviting any others, please note that I expect people who can pull their weight."

Grace's brows crashed together. "Are you talking about me?"

"No. Michaels."

Grace cleared her throat, her cheeks gaining a slight flush to them. "You don't like Brad?"

"I don't really like anyone," he replied honestly. "Except maybe you." *And Rembert.* "So if I were your older brother, I'd tell you that you could do better. He doesn't bring much to the table. I don't want to see you get hurt."

She paused, ambivalence in her expression, which was so out of character for her. In work, Grace had the tenacity of a bulldog.

"Well, you're not my brother," she said finally, her voice carrying an edge to it. "So you have no jurisdiction here, Josh. But I'll see you this afternoon." She turned and left the office.

Josh sighed. Grace probably *was* his only friend here, and now he'd managed to alienate her. Maybe he could ask Rembert to talk some sense into her.

MISSY DROVE THE BOAT—A Sea Born 26-footer with a center console—through the frothy whitecaps, her sunglasses shielding her from the bright early-afternoon sunshine and her ponytail whipping behind her. She'd been a bit surprised when McKittrick had invited her to help on his pet project, and even more surprised when he'd let her take charge of the vessel. It was the nicest one at the lab, with two 150 horsepower outboards. Brad Michaels had insisted he should captain, but McKittrick had said no. Instead, he'd handed the key to Missy, his hand warm in the exchange where his skin had brushed against hers.

Now Michaels was pouting at the front of the boat, Grace beside him. Missy ignored him.

What a beautiful day it was turning out to be. The fresh air and the sheer abandonment of flying across the water reminded her of days with her dad. And it just felt good to get out on the water during daylight. As the new girl, she'd been stuck with data entry and other tedious office jobs four days a week, and then the night shift on the long line boat for the other three. It hadn't escaped Missy's attention that Grace and McKittrick were friends, and that she had Grace to thank for this work upgrade.

McKittrick sat behind her in a wetsuit that covered his bottom half and a t-shirt protecting his torso, but he'd soon shed it. That Missy anticipated the moment only managed to annoy her. Liking McKittrick was such a bad idea.

She contemplated his Bat Suit again, currently secure on the portside of the boat. It was an open cage device that could accommodate one person, with a small motor and three air tanks, allowing the occupant to remain underwater for about three hours—chasing sharks.

Josh's goal was to swim beside the beasts to gain real-time insight into their behavior, but once he was in the water, whoever was topside was tasked with tracking him. And so far, no one had done a decent job of it.

Missy's nerves buzzed with excitement. She was definitely up to the task.

It certainly had nothing to do with McKittrick's magnetic presence, although she hadn't been able to shake the idea these past few weeks that he'd been avoiding her.

It didn't matter. It really didn't, except ... dammit, she did like him. A little too much. She'd tried hard to remain calm and cool when Grace had asked her to help him, but inside she'd jumped at the chance like a fruit fly on watermelon.

She glanced over her shoulder to check for other boats and saw McKittrick sitting beside the other girl accompanying them, his arm stretched behind her on the bench seat. Missy resumed her forward stance before they could see her mouth curl in irritation. At least her sunglasses hid the roll of her eyes.

The girl was Jen Fairfield, Missy and Grace's missing roommate. She'd been in Nassau for the past month and had returned the day before. Despite the frisson of jealousy the woman was sparking, Missy grudgingly liked her. It was clear that she and Grace were friends—the two of them talked about great white sharks like two girls gossiping about boyfriends—so Missy would befriend her, too.

But were Jen and McKittrick a thing?

Missy had gleaned from Shark Lab gossip that McKittrick didn't fool around, not even with local girls. And while he appeared friendly with Grace, it had become apparent it was nothing more than platonic.

So maybe McKittrick was just as platonic with Jen.

Or maybe he had a girlfriend back home. If that were true, then he was very devoted.

Not that any of this was Missy's business.

About five miles out, in much deeper water, Missy pulled the boat alongside a set of long lines that were maintained by the Shark Lab. Grace and Jen leaned over the gunwale to have a look.

Checking the lines was backbreaking work, and once again Missy was grateful for the sunlight—handling the sharks at night was eerie, and if she were being honest, frightening. She knew Grace, Jen, McKittrick, and Brad would need to haul each line in and check whether a shark—or something else—had been caught. Then they'd need to get vitals and quickly tag the beast before releasing it. Time was of the essence since a shark could die if it was hooked for too long. Hence, the Shark Lab had rotating shifts all day and night to check the lines.

But if a bull or tiger shark were caught, then McKittrick would get his apparatus in the water and he would follow the fish upon release as it sped away into the inky depths. Missy's job was to make sure she didn't lose McKittrick.

Missy stayed at the helm and maintained control of the boat while McKittrick and the girls began dragging up the line.

Missy frowned at Brad. "You might want to jump in and help," she said.

"They've got it covered," he replied, running a hand through his dark hair and eyeing the Bat Suit.

Missy didn't miss the scowl McKittrick cast Brad's way, but Michaels seemed oblivious to it. Grace didn't talk much about Michaels, but Missy quickly had deduced the two of them were dating. She wished she were better friends with the woman to tell her she was making a mistake. The man was lazy and always finding ways to inflate his work—which Missy had seen very little of, today being no exception—and it left a sour taste in Missy's mouth. She had to concede that the man's marginally handsome features were probably what swayed Grace, but in Missy's opinion, the man was a waste of time.

She returned her focus to her job, which was making sure the line didn't become entangled around the rotor. She sure as hell wasn't going to perform poorly today. She didn't want to give McKittrick a chance to demote her. And to be honest, she liked driving the boat more than hauling up sharks. Within a week of arriving at Shark Lab, she'd realized she no longer wanted to study sharks, but she'd kept quiet about it, since everyone here was a shark freak, and it wouldn't help her make friends. Besides, the internship would look good on the resume.

And she was in the Bahamas for the next four months, a veritable paradise. All good reasons to woman up and do the work.

The line hauling went on for the next two hours, but they found only two sharks—a black-nose and a night shark. When Missy was able to stabilize the boat, she jumped in to help the others, since they were sweating and cursing before too long. Brad finally pitched in as well.

In the late afternoon heat as the boat bobbed gently on calm waters, Missy downed a large gulp from her water bottle. They were near another long line, preparing to check it when Grace let out a squeal. A growing shadow was nearing the boat.

"Fifteen-footer," Jen said.

"Hammerhead?" Josh murmured.

Grace shifted quietly on the starboard bench where she sat on her knees and viewed the water. "Tiger," she whispered.

The reverence in all three of their voices was palpable.

Brad was busy adjusting his hat and donning mirrored sunglasses. Missy started the motor.

"Hold it steady, Missy," Josh said, hauling hard on the line, the muscles in his arms flexing.

Missy worked the throttle with as delicate of a touch as she could while keeping an eye on the shark they were trying to secure beside the boat. It was thrashing and generally uncooperative. Missy almost decided there was no way McKittrick could secure the shark with the help of only Grace and Jen—they were fit women but by no means a physical force—but she was soon proved wrong as they worked together to calm the shark by securing it beside the outer hull. Grace was near the head, somehow soothing the damned thing, and amazingly it seemed to be working. The shark calmed enough for Jen to get a measurement while Grace pulled samples for DNA, stable isotope analysis, and bloodwork, then they worked on getting the tag attached.

Maybe shark whispering really was a thing.

As they finished their assessment, McKittrick quickly went to release his Bat Suit.

"Need help?" Missy asked, since Grace and Jen were bent over the gunwale and all but cooing over the tiger shark.

"Yeah," he replied. "Cut the motor."

Missy quickly did and then joined him portside, but she couldn't help but stare at Michaels. The man had pulled a camera out of a knapsack and was snapping pictures of the Bat Suit.

"Why aren't you photographing the shark?" Missy snapped.

"This is more interesting," Brad replied. "You'll be glad later, Josh. You'll have visual documentation of your test."

"What would I do without you, Michaels?" McKittrick's tone sounded anything but grateful.

"Just trying to help."

Missy had to work hard to keep a sharp retort from flying from her mouth, since it wasn't going to help. She took a deep breath and squared her shoulders.

"You take the front end," Josh said to her. "It's lighter."

They had to pass by each other to switch positions, a tight fit that had her briefly in full body contact with him. She pretended she hadn't just committed to memory the feel and scent of him.

The Bat Suit had been secured with rope, so Missy helped release it from one end while Josh guided the heavier end that housed the motor. Together, they lowered it as Brad's camera clicked away.

"Brad, you mind helping Missy hold it while I get ready?" he asked.

"It's fine," Missy said. "I've got it."

Brad grinned. "She's got it."

She was glad her hands were busy, otherwise she would've grabbed Brad's camera and tossed it into the ocean.

McKittrick tore off his t-shirt, revealing lean muscle and a smattering of chest hair. He pulled on his wetsuit and zipped the back, then quickly donned a scuba mask and tank. He didn't need flippers since there was a motor. He slipped into the water, climbed inside the cage, and Missy latched it shut. He put the regulator in his mouth, started the motor, then gave a thumb's up, and Missy returned the gesture. She released the final rope securing the cage, and it sank into the depths.

"He's in the water," Missy said.

"Copy," Grace said. "Releasing the shark now."

Grace and Jen loosened the rope they'd been using to secure the tiger against the hull. As the massive creature swam away, Missy noted the bubbles from McKittrick's regulator. Without taking her eyes off him, she went back to the captain's seat, started the motor, and gently eased the boat away from the long lines.

The afternoon turned into a huge success, at least for McKittrick. He was able to trail the shark for over two hours while Missy kept tabs on him, constantly watching the surface. She soon became accustomed to the telltale signs from his apparatus, as well as the bubbles from his scuba gear. When he finally surfaced, she was right beside him.

But when they returned to base, they faced a ticked-off Ruth, the Station Manager.

"How long were you away from the lines?" she asked, hands on hips, her tan face marred into a frown. Missy had trouble pegging the woman's age, but the gray hair gave her a matronly air.

"About two hours," McKittrick said, adjusting a ballcap over hair that clearly had not been cut in a while. A hazard of island life, Missy guessed.

"You missed two sharks," she said.

"We checked all the lines," Grace said, coming forward. "We found four, including the tiger. They must've gotten hooked after we left. If you're angry, blame me. I was the dive master on this shift. I gave McKittrick permission to get in the water."

Ruth shifted her gaze between the two. "Well, you're lucky the next shift found them—a juvenile hammerhead and a ten-foot bull."

"Did they make it?" Missy asked.

"They did." Ruth pressed her mouth together in a sour expression. She sighed. "Josh, you can't use your apparatus on normal shifts. Even Grace does her sonar testing with the lemons in her off-time."

"What are you saying?" he asked.

"You'll have to accompany other shifts if you want to swim around after the sharks."

Irritation crossed his features. "So now I have to do double the work *and* find another boat to transport my suit?"

Ruth crossed her arms. "We're not here for your pet projects. Right, Grace?"

Grace's face showed what she thought of that policy, which explained why she'd probably helped Josh in the first place.

"We're here to study and catalogue sharks," Ruth continued. Before McKittrick could interrupt, she added, "Our way. Follow our policy or go home." She turned and went back into the office.

"Well, shit," McKittrick said. He pulled off the ballcap and ran a hand through his salt encrusted hair.

Jen slung a pack on her shoulder. "You just need to find another boat, Josh."

"Yeah, but where I am gonna do that?"

She shrugged and walked toward the cabins.

"I might have a solution," Missy said.

The look McKittrick gave her was filled with speculation and if she weren't mistaken, a hint of wanting. But maybe it was just for the boat. Still, her heart sped up, and she began to sweat a little more beyond what the late day heat was causing.

If she could get him a boat, would he reward her with … stop. It was annoying how much she liked the approval in his eyes, even if it was just for his project.

CHAPTER 5

Present Day

Since their meal was finished—Josh had insisted on paying despite Missy protesting—they both stood, and she walked over to Brad Michaels. She didn't recognize the other two men with him.

"Hey, Brad," she said. His dark hair was trimmed a little too short and his normally compact body looked a bit out of shape.

Brad's surprise seemed real. "Missy? What a small world." Then his eyes flicked behind her. "Josh." Brad laughed. "This is wild. Are you guys back together?"

"Just work," Missy said.

"Here on Abaco?" Brad asked.

Missy thought she caught a nervous twitch in the man's eyes.

She nodded. "Why are you here?" She spread her gaze to include the other two men.

"This is Mike and Wyatt," Brad said. "We're on a rescue project."

No one bothered to shake hands.

"Who are you working for?" Josh asked.

"Sink or Swim Salvage."

Missy held her surprise in check. She'd known Brad had left

CMI after butting heads with his ex, Grace, over her shark array apparatus, and Missy had been happy about it. He'd all but stolen Grace's work and had tried to pass it off as his own; he deserved to be fired. While Missy wasn't surprised he'd found another job, she was taken aback that he would end up at a place like Sink or Swim. The company had a dubious reputation. He'd sunk lower than she could've hoped, and by all accounts it should've made her happy, but something about it felt off.

Josh beat her to the next question. "Why is a salvage company on a rescue mission?" he asked.

"There was an incident in a blue hole off the coast," Brad said. "A diver named Howie Barrett was killed about six months ago and his body was never recovered."

"And you're here to retrieve it?" Missy asked.

"Yep."

Her hopes plummeted. They would all be diving in the same place.

She turned to Josh and said in a low voice, "I thought Ken had the only permit."

Brad must have heard. "Oh, you guys are here on the exploration team?" But he seemed about as happy as they were about the prospect of working in the same location. "Our permit is for body retrieval. The family wants some closure. The Bahamian government didn't think it would interfere with your work, so they gave us permission."

"The hell it won't interfere," Josh cut in. "You'll be in our fucking way. And body retrieval is dangerous. You should tell the family he's better off staying where he is, or one of you might die."

Mike and Wyatt appeared to shrug off the assessment of their skills, and Brad smirked. "These guys are good. We know what we're doing. We'll stay clear of you, but alert us if you see anything. You know, like a dead body."

Josh shook his head. "This is bullshit. Let's talk to Ken."

Missy nodded. "See you around, Brad," she said and followed Josh from the restaurant.

They went to the lobby where Missy's gear was stacked off to the side with the others' and met up with Ken, Sarah, Andy, and Lucy. Josh quickly caught everyone up on the situation.

Ken sighed. "No, I didn't know about a second permit. I'd been assured we'd have the hole to ourselves for ten days. I'll make some calls." He headed to a phone in the lobby.

Josh extracted himself from the group. Missy watched as he went to his equipment and began checking on it. She found it oddly endearing that Josh was still Josh—never very chatty and generally avoiding social situations that didn't revolve around work. It reminded her of the first time she'd ever seen him, tinkering on his Bat Suit on a sweltering day in Bimini. He still possessed the same intense focus that once had been directed at her. It had been a hell of a thing—heady, exhilarating, the most fun she'd ever had. And then reality had crashed through the dream when she and her mom had lost her dad, and Missy hadn't been able to believe she could have that moment back with Josh. Instead, she'd tried to accept that having had it at all was enough.

Trying to ignore the painful longing radiating from her abdomen to her chest for a man who was no longer hers, she left the lobby and found Brad in the atrium alone.

"How's Grace doing?" he asked.

"So much better without you," she replied honestly.

"Your dislike of me was always unwarranted. All I ever wanted was to get Grace's project off the ground. And I did."

Missy frowned. "You're seriously going to take credit for it?"

"It's just business."

"Right. And now you're in the salvage business. You're really going places, Brad."

He narrowed his eyes. "Still playing with octopus?"

"They're definitely better company than most people."

He nodded. "Josh McKittrick is a lost cause. He always was."

She laughed. "This coming from you?"

"Nah. From you. You dumped him after you left Shark Lab. Obviously you wised up."

Talking to Brad had been a mistake, she realized now. He'd always had a knack for putting her into a foul mood.

"I think you're confusing me for you," she said. "Grace dumped *you*."

"That's not true. I left *her*."

God, why did she bother speaking to him?

The concierge approached them. "Mr. Michaels?"

"Yes," Brad replied.

"I've got you all booked on the rum tour this afternoon. A shuttle will pick you up in an hour out front."

"Thanks." Brad took the brochure from the man. "Excuse me, Missy. I've got better things to do."

As he walked away, Missy's attention landed on the small bar adjacent to the lobby. She ordered a ginger ale and took her time drinking it. She could've used something stronger, but Brad's afternoon of sightseeing had given her an idea. One that meant she needed to be clearheaded.

Once her blood pressure was under control, she returned to the team at the same time as Ken.

"Unfortunately, I didn't get anywhere," he said. "We're stuck sharing the hole with them."

"We need to drop Benji today," Josh said, referring to his deep-diving apparatus.

"That wasn't the plan, Josh," Ken said. "Today's outing was just recon on the hole. We aren't diving below thirty feet."

Josh shook his head in disagreement. "We need to amend that. We need to get Benji on the bottom."

"I agree," Missy said. "I just spoke with Brad Michaels, who's on the other team, and they're not going out today. We need to take advantage of that."

Ken looked around at everyone. "Okay. Is everyone up for a deep dive on day one?"

"Let's do it," Sarah said with enthusiasm.

Andy and Lucy gave a nod, but it was half-hearted at best. Missy knew they were the least experienced with deep dives.

"I'll help Josh position his equipment," Missy said.

He eyed her. "You up for that?" he asked. "It'll be deep."

"It's my job to keep an eye on you. You're not going down there alone, McKittrick."

"The boat I reserved won't work—it's too small for Benji," Ken said. "Let me see if I can get a different one. I'm calling in all my favors on day one. No hiccups, okay?" He looked at everyone.

Missy went to her room to grab her rebreather. Time to use her training.

CHAPTER 6

Four years ago …

Josh followed Missy into Alice Town, located in North Bimini. It was the nearest stop for shops, restaurants, and bars. For a new girl, she appeared confident about her destination. She wore a sun visor and sunglasses, her brown hair swept back into a ponytail. Jean shorts revealed tan legs and her dark green camp shirt hinted at the curves beneath. Hell, it couldn't be much more distracting if she were parading around in a bikini.

Now he had visions of her in a bikini.

Shit.

He focused on her feet. He had a thing for feet, but hers were clad in a white pair of sneakers with no socks. It was good she wasn't wearing flip flops.

He bumped into a man going the other way on the busy street known as The King's Highway.

"Sorry," Josh said.

He shifted his gaze forward. *Stop getting distracted.*

"Where are we going?" he said, not meaning to bark out the question. He pulled a bag of gummy bears from his pocket and popped a few in his mouth.

She cast him an annoyed look—at least he thought it was annoyed since he couldn't see her eyes behind the mirrored sunglasses.

He offered her some of his candy, and she took a few.

"Thanks," she said, her tone softening. "We're almost there."

"I apologize for my gruffness," he said, trying to make amends, which he usually never did. He didn't much care what the other interns—the Labbers—thought of him.

She slowed her pace so he could walk beside her.

"Having a bad day?" she asked. "You seem to have a lot of those."

"Why do you say that?"

Her lips formed a barely-there smile. "Never mind."

They came to a dive shop. A bell jingled as she pulled open the front door. It was like most of the local haunts—a bit cluttered with scuba gear and boogie boards, a fan buzzing behind the narrow counter. Missy approached and hit the bell with a loud ding. An older Bahamian appeared, wiping his hands with a rag. As soon as he saw her his face split into a wide grin, revealing white teeth.

"Missy!" His voice was clipped with the accent of most locals.

"Billy!"

He came around the counter and gave her a big hug, which she returned in equal measure.

"Your father said you were coming to the islands," Billy said.

"It's good to see you." She stepped back. "This is Josh McKittrick. He's also at Shark Lab." She looked back at the man who was obviously a close friend. "This is Billy Demeritte."

Josh shook the man's hand. "It's nice to meet you." Then he said to Missy, "So you've been to Bimini before?"

"When I was younger, with my dad."

"George Rembert came often," Billy said. "Tell him we miss him. We've got plenty of grouper to go around."

Missy smiled warmly. "I will."

Billy raised an eyebrow. "But you did not come by to say hello only. You looking for a charter?"

"You read my mind."

Billy gave her a side-look. "And why am I thinking you're looking for something cheap …."

"If by cheap you mean free, then that would be a yes."

Billy paused for a moment, contemplating. "I could probably find you something. How big?"

Missy glanced at Josh and shrugged. "Twenty-six feet with double outboard motors?"

Billy laughed. "I'm glad to see you haven't lost your sense of humor. I remember when you couldn't see past this counter. You were a happy one, I'll give you that. Always laughing, always squealing."

Missy seemed a bit embarrassed by Billy's reminiscing, but Josh rather liked the idea of a wild little girl with free abandon.

"I can give you a sixteen-foot skiff," Billy said. "How long you need it for?"

"Three or four days?" Missy replied, directing the question at Josh, who nodded.

"What's it for? Are you two on a romantic adventure?"

"What?" Missy exclaimed. "No."

Man, she didn't even hesitate. Her swift denial briefly crushed him, but maybe she was already involved with someone on the mainland. But how serious?

"McKittrick is testing an underwater apparatus to swim after sharks, and the lab is being stingy with their boats."

Billy sighed and planted his hands loosely on his hips. "Then you'll need something bigger than the skiff. The currents in the gulf stream'll beat you up." He paused, contemplating. "I'll have to rearrange some charters, but I've got a bay boat, twenty feet. That should work."

"Thank you." She leaned forward and kissed Billy on the cheek. "You're the best."

"My wife will want to see you." He looked at Josh and winked as he added, "And your work friend."

Josh didn't bother to correct the man on thinking that he and Missy were an item. He rather liked the implication.

"Of course," Missy said. "I don't have much free time at the moment, but maybe in a few weeks."

Billy nodded. "I'll call over to the Lab when I've got you square with the boat."

"Appreciate it," Josh said.

"Well, you should." Billy returned a speculative glare. "Missy's like family. She must like you to stick her neck out like this."

MISSY WALKED MORE SLOWLY beside McKittrick as they headed down the street through town. For a moment, she was tongue-tied. Billy had all but said how much she liked McKittrick, and while it was true, she didn't need McKittrick to know about it.

"Just for the record, I'm sticking my neck out for you because I think your project is cool," she said, trying to clear the air.

"Don't worry," McKittrick answered. "I never once thought you liked me."

"That would be true," she teased. "I'm just trying to get out of scrubbing the office floor."

McKittrick chuckled. "Good luck with that. We've all had to take a turn. So you're not a Bimini virgin like most of the interns?"

"Nah. My dad loves this place. It was one of the reasons I applied to Shark Lab." She slipped her thumbs into her back pockets as they walked.

"It was nice of you to go to bat for me."

"You're welcome. But, of course, you know it means I get to drive the boat. I'm your partner now. No cutting me out."

"There's no money in this, Missy."

"I know. But I'd hate to see you as a shark snack one day."

"Thanks for the vote of confidence," he said.

"Just keeping it real."

"All right, I owe you one."

She cocked an eyebrow. "Really?"

He glanced at her. "And I'll tell you how I'm gonna repay you."

Her stomach did a somersault, and her mouth went dry. If he asked her on a date, a yes was primed and ready at the tip of her tongue.

"I'll help you find the rum."

"Come again?"

"You haven't heard about the rum bottle?"

She shook her head.

His lips spread into a wide smile, and Missy swallowed past the dry mouth again.

"You'll find out tonight," he added.

And with that, he refused to say more.

BRAD MICHAELS HANDED Missy a hand-drawn map encompassing the Bimini chain—South, North, and East Bimini Islands—scribbled with symbols and clues.

"You've got to be kidding me," she murmured.

McKittrick hadn't been joking. It turned out the new kid in town, or rather the newest intern to arrive at the Lab, was tasked with finding a hidden bottle of rum, an initiation of sorts.

"Good luck." Brad smirked, leaning close, to which Missy took a step back. She couldn't fathom why Grace liked the guy. The way he casually flirted with Missy—and some of the other girls present—had her doubting his ability to be faithful.

She had to stuff down the impulse to say *yuck* to his face.

McKittrick suddenly appeared, giving Missy a bit of whiplash as he inserted his tall frame between her and Brad. He was so close that she could smell the soap he had obviously used recently, since the balmy and salty tropical air kept everyone nice and sweaty most of the time. Once Brad was forced to retreat from Missy's personal space, McKittrick did the same, and damned if she didn't wish he would stay. The difference between him and Brad was night and day.

McKittrick was quiet and never boasted. Whenever Missy crossed paths with him, he was always engrossed in work, whether it be at his laptop or working on his Bat Suit or fixing whatever needed to be fixed around the lab—generators, boat motors, the rusty vehicles the local staff used. Brad, on the other hand, was overly interested in everyone else's projects, especially Grace's very basic shark sonar array she was developing. Missy vowed to help her friend out more often, if only to keep Brad away.

"I see you have the map," McKittrick said, grabbing a beer from the cooler. It was Friday night and everyone at the Lab was crowded into the small dining area. Rather than keep the beer for himself, McKittrick offered it to her.

She took it. "Thanks."

She was about to set the map down to open the can when McKittrick leaned forward and did it for her, brushing her hand in the process.

"Don't let go of that," he said, referring to the map. "It's too valuable to risk losing."

She held up the paper. "You think this is valuable? It looks like a six-year-old drew it."

McKittrick cocked an eyebrow and said quietly, "Brad was in charge this time."

"That explains it, then." She didn't hide the sarcasm in her voice, enjoying a secret exchange with McKittrick as his gaze danced with amusement.

Grace appeared from the crowd, Jen beside her. "Oh good, you have it," she said, looking at the paper in Missy's hand.

McKittrick pulled two more beers and handed them to the girls, but Missy noted that he didn't open them as he had for her.

"Are you ready?" Jen asked.

Missy frowned. "I suppose. Is there a time limit?"

"Of course. You must find it tonight."

"In the dark?" Missy asked. The sun would set in a few hours, and she doubted she could finish her search before darkness arrived. She took a swig of beer. This was looking to be a long night.

"I think there's a flashlight around here somewhere," Grace said.

Missy looked at McKittrick. "Do I still get to cash in that favor?"

Grace and Jen both stared at the man.

"You're going to help her?" Grace asked.

McKittrick didn't answer, instead taking a drink of beer from the can he'd finally retrieved for himself.

"You didn't help me," Grace added.

"Or me," Jen chimed in.

"How long did it take each of you to find it?" Missy inquired.

"About six hours," Jen said. "Grace, however, has the worst record ever," she added with a laugh.

Grace's face scrunched in frustration. "I wasted too much time trying to write a computer program to cross reference the handmade map to this side of Bimini."

"You're such a nerd, Grace," McKittrick said under his breath.

"Grease monkey," she shot back.

"Anyway," Jen cut in, "Grace spent half the night digging holes over at Bimini Sands Beach. That's when the police showed up."

Grace shook her head. "I got a citation for vandalizing the beach. I had to wait two days before I could resume my search while making sure I didn't get into trouble."

"Is it against the rules for McKittrick to help me?" Missy asked.

Grace shrugged. "If you don't mind being hazed about it, then no."

McKittrick's attention focused across the room where Samson and Delilah had just run in and were yipping at no one in particular. "Those mutts need a walk," he said, then looked at Missy. "Meet me out back in an hour." He retrieved the dogs and left.

Grace and Jen huddled closer to her to block out the noise of the various conversations in the room.

"What's the skinny with Josh?" Jen asked.

"What do you mean?" Missy knew what Jen meant but felt she needed to tread lightly.

"Are you two a thing?"

Missy couldn't tell if Jen was curious, jealous, or annoyed. "Would it bother you if we were?"

Jen's eyes widened in surprise. "Oh no, of course not. I'm not into Josh."

Missy shifted her attention to Grace, a questioning look on her face.

"Not me, either," Grace replied. "I'm with Brad, remember?" She frowned at each of them as if they should be more supportive of her relationship status, giving Missy a pang of remorse for her uncharitable thoughts about Brad. It wasn't her place to tell Grace who she should date.

"Sorry if it seems like we're interrogating you," Grace continued. "We're both friends with Josh, nothing more. We're just surprised."

"Why?" Missy wondered if she should be offended. But the truth was, she had no idea if McKittrick was interested in her. While she felt a frisson of something from him at times, he otherwise kept any interest on lockdown.

"He's never hooked up with anyone while we've been here," Jen said. "We're just surprised he finally caved."

Missy felt she needed to clear the air. "Listen, it's not like that. I mean, he's not made a move."

"I think he has," Grace said. "He's offering to find the rum with you. That's a date."

Missy's brows crashed together, but a wave of nerves tickled her abdomen. "That's not the feeling I'm getting from him."

"You should go for it," Jen said. "Unless you have a boyfriend back home?"

"No," Missy replied. "What about Josh? Is he single?"

"Yep," Grace said. "His last girlfriend was sometime last year, but they broke up months ago, before he ever came here."

Missy took a deep breath. "All right, any advice on how to proceed?"

"Well, the most important thing is don't let him come across a broken motor or something," Grace said.

"Yeah," Jen said, laughing. "He'll get distracted, and your date will be over before it started."

"And don't go skinny dipping."

"Why?" Missy asked.

"Well, aside from the fact that it's illegal," Grace replied, "you'll never live it down."

JOSH LET Missy take charge of the search for the rum bottle since the point was an initiation of sorts for the new intern. Still, Brad's crappy map had Josh grinding his teeth, and he almost took over a few times, but then the evening might have ended too soon. And the truth was, Josh liked having Missy to himself.

"Based on my survey of the other interns," Missy said, "the bottle has almost always been buried on a beach." She tucked her loose hair behind her ear as she looked at the map. She wore a navy blouse tucked into faded jeans that molded to her hips, and Josh tried to keep from wondering how those hips would fit against his.

She looked up, squinting into the setting sun. They had been walking along Radio Beach, and with the breeze and the late day sun casting Missy in an ethereal glow, Josh thought he might start spouting poetry at any moment.

"I'm guessing you think the bottle isn't on the beach." He put his hands in the pockets of his khaki shorts, sidestepping a pile of seaweed and bumping shoulders with her.

"I need to think like Brad," she said, her eyes filled with amusement. "A stretch, I know. I figure he's gone two ways with this. He wants me to *think* it's on a beach. As we can see from the map, he's left off many landmarks including the ocean. This just proves he's a prick for the fun of it. Or it *is* on a beach because he truly is too lazy to come up with something original. That brings me full circle to my prick comment."

Josh smiled. "I can tell you the brand of rum used," he said, "and we could buy a bottle. Then we could spend the evening eating fish burgers and drinking beer."

She regarded him. "Very tempting, but I'll not be accused of cheating. I do have a reputation to uphold." Her eyes dropped back to the map, and she shook her head slightly. "I actually think this section here"—she pointed to the right side of the paper—"is a neighborhood. Let's get off the beach."

"Whatever you say, Boss."

As they began walking, she asked, "How long have you been here?"

"About eight months now."

"Will you be finishing up soon?"

He nodded. "Next month."

"That's soon." He thought he heard an echo of regret in her voice. "Where's home?"

"Melbourne, Florida. I'm getting my Ph.D. at Florida Tech. If you're ever in town, look me up."

"I will," she replied.

"What are your plans after your stint here?" he asked.

"Well, don't tell anybody, but I've decided shark research isn't to my taste. I've been at USC, but I'd like to go somewhere else for my doctorate, so I suppose I'll have to figure it all out in the next few months. Hopefully the change won't cost me more time at school."

Josh considered her confession. "You might be the first person at Shark Lab to lose interest in sharks after coming here."

"Maybe. I think meeting Grace and Jen showed me what true passion and devotion to the fish looks like. I don't have that."

"But you're a natural on the water. Did you spend a lot of time fishing with your dad?"

"I did. He instilled a love of the ocean in me. It's my happy place. I guess I thought studying sharks sounded glamorous and that's why I picked it as a discipline, but I prefer quieter moments in the water, not feeling stressed out worrying about the top predator bumping into me."

"Don't tell the orcas you said that."

She shrugged. "True." She pointed at a bar they were approaching. "See that sign?" She pulled the map from her back pocket, drawing Josh's gaze once again to her athletic curves. "Brad put an octopus here. I think it might mean this place."

Josh glanced at the sign above. "The Eight-Legged Mollusk?"

"It's close enough." She opened the door and went inside.

It was a well-worn local joint that Josh had never been to. They settled at the bar.

"What can I get you?" Josh asked her.

"The local amber is fine."

He ordered two, and the bartender delivered them a few minutes later.

Missy took a sip and glanced around. "Where do you think it is?"

"I'm gonna go with your assessment of Brad's laziness and guess it's somewhere in the open."

"I say we finish our drinks first," she said, lifting her glass. Josh clinked his against it.

Her gaze dropped to the long scar on his arm. It ran from his wrist to his elbow.

"What's the story with that?" she asked. "Shark attack?"

"Nothing that grand. My older brother sliced me open with a machete."

She sputtered the beer she had just swallowed and coughed. "What? That sounds horrible." She set her glass down. "How old were you?"

"About twelve, I suppose."

"What on earth were you doing with a machete?"

"My mom and dad were gearing up to head down to South America, and it was in the stuff they were taking. Chris decided we should go in the back yard and practice our hacking skills. We lived in Phoenix and my dad had let the yard go, so there was a lot of very tall, dry grass. It was an accident. My brother didn't see me."

Missy's eyes were wide, and her mouth hung open. "How many stitches?"

"One hundred and twenty-three."

"Shit," she whispered under her breath. "Your mom must've been beside herself."

"Well, once I was patched up, she left on her trip, so she got over it pretty quick."

"Why were your parents going to South America?"

"They're geologists," he said. "It was a work trip."

"Huh. Cool. Did you ever travel with them?"

"Yeah, a few times, but my mom didn't like Chris and me to miss too much school. My grandmother would come and stay when both my folks had to leave at the same time."

"Your grandmother must've been a tough woman," she said.

"She was. She was a cop in her younger days."

"Impressive."

"Chris and I rarely misbehaved around her. I sometimes wonder if my parents left us with her on purpose."

"To whip you into shape?"

He drained the beer in his glass. "Something like that. I got my love of mechanics from her."

"I really didn't expect this."

"What's that?" he asked.

"Meeting a guy who has such strong women in his life."

"I'm perfect boyfriend material," he said, while he flagged the bartender for another beer.

"That's not what I've been hearing."

He smiled, enjoying the banter. "You've been asking about me?"

Missy narrowed her eyes. "Maybe. But then I also asked about Brad."

"I've been told he's cute."

She pulled a bowl of peanuts closer and popped a few in her mouth. "Cute like a con artist. I'm worried about Grace."

"Grace is a big girl. She can take care of herself."

"She's too distracted by her shark array, and I think Brad takes advantage of that."

"What would you do if your friends told you the guy you liked was bad news?"

She laughed. "Are we talking about Brad or you now?"

He frowned. "Who said I was bad news? And you like me?"

The look in her eyes was his answer.

"Let's find this rum," he said, "and then I'll take you to the best kept secret on Bimini."

With decisiveness, she finished her drink and waved the bartender over once again. "Did a man with dark hair and an adorable face that hides his slimy nature come in here and ask to leave a bottle of rum?"

The female bartender smiled. "Oh yeah."

CHAPTER 7

Present Day

The blue hole was about ten nautical miles offshore, so Missy spent the ride getting her rebreather gear in order and running through a checklist in her head. Josh, Ken, and Sarah were also preparing themselves, but Andy and Lucy would be using only scuba as neither of them were rated for rebreathers.

Usually, blue holes were isolated in the interior of an island and filled with fresh water, but with this one they would have to contend with ocean currents as well as salt water.

The boat Ken had hired had a small crane. Once they were in position near the hole, the captain dropped anchor, and Josh, Ken and Andy worked to get Benji connected to the crane.

They all entered the water as Benji was lowered and detached, with Missy and Josh taking the lead. Sarah and Ken would back them up, while Andy and Lucy would keep watch until one hundred feet—the limits of scuba—then they would proceed with preliminary scouting of the hole.

The benthic lander was autonomous, so Josh easily guided the descent as they moved along the edge of the blue hole. Marine life was abundant, with coral such as Elkhorn and brain corals, black-tipped reef sharks, stingrays, and clams. A New Providence cusk-eel poked its head out and a Caribbean reef octopus quickly camouflaged itself. Shrimp, neon gobies, angelfish, groupers, and purple sea fans filled the scenery. It was an oasis, and breathtaking in its beauty. The sea never ceased to amaze Missy.

As they entered the center of the hole, an inky blue darkness enveloped them, and they switched on their dive lights mounted beside their masks. They continued their descent, and Missy scanned for obstacles while keeping an eye on her depth gauge.

At one hundred feet, Andy and Lucy broke away. Missy changed her regulator from her tank of nitrox to the second tank strapped to her back. It contained heliox since deep dives required different breathing mixtures to eliminate oxygen toxicity. She confirmed the rest of the team did the same.

At one-hundred-seventy feet they hit the halocline, the place where dense saltwater mixed with fresh water, creating a murky layer of hydrogen sulfide gas. Josh stopped Benji's descent and hovered in place.

"I'll check it out," Missy said.

"Roger that," Josh replied. "Be careful."

Missy braced herself to pass through the sulfide layer. Although she was covered from head to toe in neoprene, some divers had reported burning skin or stomach cramps. Down she went.

While there had been an abundance of life near the surface, and less so as they'd descended, below the sulfide layer there was nothing, as if it were a version of the moon underwater. There was no oxygen below the sulfide, so nothing could live here, at least nothing carbon-based. One of Benji's goals, Josh had told her, was to take water and core samples to determine if some other type of life existed here, possibly mimicking conditions that would be present on another planet.

Missy paused for a moment and took in the surroundings, turning in the water to direct the light from her headlamp to give her a visual. They weren't at the bottom. Yet. She rose back to the others.

"All clear," she said.

They continued with their descent. At one-hundred-ninety-five feet the benthic layer—the bottom—became visible. Very carefully, the four of them guided Benji to a landing position, settling it onto a debris field and stirring up sediment.

Once the silt had settled, Josh said, "Firing up the lander." It had been on minimal power, but now that it was positioned, he activated the remainder of Benji's systems.

"I'm going to take two core samples before we leave," he added.

While he did that, the rest of them tentatively explored the area, entering an enclosure.

"Stalactites," Missy said, looking at the protruding rocky formations.

"Proving once again this was a cave system before the last ice age," Ken said. Bright flashes accompanied his camera as he took photos.

Sarah's flipper caught one of the stalactites, and it completely disintegrated, crashing to the ocean floor, and creating another cloud of silt.

"Sorry," Sarah said. "This environment is fragile."

"Remain where you are," Missy said.

"We all need to be more careful," Ken said.

"Agreed," Missy replied.

When visibility returned, Josh had joined them. "Let's go," he said.

"You don't have to tell me twice," Sarah said. "It's too eerie down here."

"I find it rather peaceful," Josh said.

Missy smiled to herself, silently agreeing.

JOSH WAS tired as they arrived at the hotel, night falling. Ken told the driver to go to the rear of the resort. They had most of their gear with them since they would use a different boat until it was time to retrieve Benji, so the hotel had given them a storage room to house all their stuff, not wanting it to be an eyesore in the lobby.

It had been a long afternoon, but he was relieved that Benji was deployed, and everything appeared to be going well with the lander. This was the first real test for the device, and he owed Ken for bringing him on board and giving him a chance to test the design.

And then there was Missy. Despite everything, he enjoyed working beside her. He always had. Sharing his work, even if it was just as friends, was more fun than any other relationship he'd attempted since she'd left him.

Frustration pushed at him.

He didn't want to be her friend. He'd known that five minutes after they'd met all those years ago.

Missy had exited the van and was talking to Sarah when her attention veered to the right. He followed her gaze.

Was that …?

She started walking toward the apparatus that had caught her attention, and he fell into step beside her as the others dropped their gear into the storage room. Her shoulder gently bumped against his, and he didn't pull away.

"Is that your Bat Suit?" she whispered.

It sure looked like it. A large, elongated cage was secured on a trailer with an extension cord plugged into a large battery pack on the back end and running to a hotel outlet.

They both saw the logo affixed to a metal plate at the same time: Sink or Swim Salvage.

"Sonofabitch," Missy said. "It figures it would be Brad Michaels. Did you give this to him?"

"No."

She turned to him. "Did *you* bring this?"

"No, of course not."

"So he stole it?"

"Not necessarily."

"But surely you protected your work. You have a patent or something, don't you?"

Josh didn't answer, instead inspecting the latch mechanism on the cage door. He sighed, considering the implications.

Missy met his gaze from across the cage. "Talk to me, McKittrick."

He ran a hand through his hair. "I was waiting until I got to a more final prototype because there'd been issues with the impeller, the battery, and the door latch."

"It's been four years," she said, the incredulity obvious in her voice. "What the hell have you been doing all this time?"

Thinking about you.

He couldn't possibly explain why he'd shelved the project because the truth was that after she'd left him, he'd had trouble getting back to his life, and that damned Bat Suit had reminded him too much of his time with her. It hadn't been a conscious effort to abandon the design, there were just always other projects to focus on. A month turned into a year which turned into four years.

He tried to get his mind back on track with the job at hand and not the fact that Missy Rembert was suddenly back in his life, all flesh-and-blood woman, wreaking havoc on his concentration.

"I had other things to work on," he said. "And we don't know that Brad stole it. A motorized diving cage is a general design. I don't want to make a scene and screw things up for Ken."

"Didn't you ever hear what Brad did to Grace?"

"No."

"He took her shark array prototype idea to CMI to get hired. And the asshole ended up being her boss."

"You're kidding."

"I wish I were," she said. "Her concept was open-sourced, so he wasn't violating any law by stealing it and passing it off as his own, except showing what a smarmy little worm he was. But she managed to get the last laugh. She copyrighted her deep learning computer algorithm, and she made a deal with the CMI bigwigs that if it worked, they'd give her full credit for the apparatus. She managed to get Brad pushed out in the process."

"I had no idea Grace could be so ruthless. Good for her."

"It doesn't come naturally. I may have prodded her along when she faltered."

Josh should be happy that Missy and Grace had remained friends, but he wasn't prepared for the stab of jealousy the news inflicted. Missy had apparently stayed in contact with everyone *but* him. It tore at the wound left behind when she'd departed his life, just enough to draw a drop or two of blood.

He hid his reaction by looking at the apparatus more closely.

"What is it?" she asked.

For a moment, he thought she was asking how he felt about her leaving him, but then he realized the question was about the cage. It was just as well they didn't reopen the wound. There was no point. When this expedition was over, they would go their separate ways.

He fell back on work, like he always had.

"Some of the design is mine," he said.

"What parts?"

"The latch mechanism. If you recall, I had trouble with it."

She nodded. "I remember."

"I changed it later." *Before I abandoned the cage altogether.* "And he's using a lead-acid battery," he continued, "although that's not necessarily a theft of my idea. But there can be problems with those under pressure. The impeller, however, looks just like mine. I had trouble with that too."

"Serves him right then. He stole an early design and never bothered to upgrade it. Brad Michaels has never had an original thought in his life."

"I can't disagree," Josh said. "I'm sure he'll deny lifting the design, but I should probably warn him about some of the problems."

"You're a lot nicer than I am. Let him rot in the thing." She grimaced. "Sorry. I really need to work on being a team player, I guess."

"You're a team player, Missy. I'm glad to have you watching my six in the water." And that was the truth. Maybe if he'd said more of it back then, she wouldn't have run from him and never looked back.

Her face softened. "Thanks."

Reluctantly, he turned back to their gear that was still sitting where it had been dropped by the van driver. "We should get cleaned up for dinner."

"Yep. Right."

He'd been this close to making a play for her. And that was stupid. Because if she rejected him again, it would not only ruin the expedition, it would break his heart all over again.

"You're with Josh?" Grace asked, her voice filled with surprise on the other end of the line.

"Yes," Missy replied, tamping down her frustration as she switched her cellphone to her other ear. She'd just told Grace about Brad's unexpected presence on Abaco and the possibility that he'd stolen someone else's work yet again, and all Grace could fixate on was McKittrick's reappearance in Missy's life. Not that Missy wasn't fixating on it herself, but she had hoped to keep her turmoil to herself.

"What's that like?" Grace asked.

"I'm not sure what you mean."

"I mean, are sparks flying between you two?"

"No," Missy answered but it was a lie. "Everything is fine."

"Really?"

"Of course."

"You do remember that I was with Josh in Bimini after you left. I saw how worried he was about you after you lost your dad. I saw how heartsick when you cut him loose."

Missy took a deep breath. "Well, that's all in the past now."

"Okay." But Grace didn't sound convinced.

Time to steer the conversation back to Missy's real reason for calling her best friend. "What should we do about Brad?"

"Well, I think it's pretty obvious."

"What is?"

"Night dives."

Missy made a sound of acknowledgment.

"You don't like that idea?" Grace asked.

"I don't love night diving."

"Since when?"

Missy didn't respond.

"You know," Grace said, "I'm beginning to take offense at how much you've kept from me over the years." But her tone wasn't argumentative, more like an older sister lecturing her sibling. "You've been night diving before, so I know you can do this. Josh certainly can. As for the others on your team, I'm not overly familiar with them so you'll just have to ask. And Brad, well … don't let him suck the joy from your work. We know he excels at it but remember, I used to date him. If I can get past his assholery, then you can too. Try to keep him in the rearview mirror and get out there and kick butt in that blue hole. I'm excited by what you might find, so you'd better share every detail with me when you return.

"And finally, McKittrick," she added. "That's what's really throwing you off. To be honest, I've always wondered why you've never been able to settle down with any other guy, and if you want my opinion, it's because of Josh. You've been handed an opportunity to clear the air with him, and I think you should take it. It'll be good for the soul. Is he with someone?"

"Here? No."

"Elsewhere?" Grace asked.

"I'm not sure."

"Aha." Grace laughed. "I can hear it in your voice. He's getting to you. I'm not sure why you left him and why you did it so badly, but you need to make amends."

"God, you're annoying."

"Just looking out for you. Josh was always one of my favorites from Bimini. Tell him I said hi."

"And he says hi back. He was very happy to hear you were no longer with Brad. Speaking of which, how is cohabitation going with Galloway?"

"Good so far."

Grace and her filmmaker boyfriend, Alec Galloway, had moved in together about three weeks ago.

"And he's okay living in your house and in your town?" Missy asked.

Alec had been in San Mateo, up north near San Francisco, not far from Missy, with Grace being in Monterey, about a four-hour drive away. She had a cute house in Pacific Grove, and after she and Alec had begun their whirlwind romance while on an expedition in Baja Mexico, they'd been trying to date long distance. Missy hadn't been too surprised when Alec had decided to move south to be with Grace—he was head over heels for her—but still, Missy had had a knot of worry in her stomach.

She'd thought it was for Grace, but now she had to concede that the commitment was making her vicariously nervous. And it all stemmed back to Josh.

"Yeah, he's loving it, I think," Grace said. "And I have to say it's nice waking up to his sexy mug every morning."

"He hasn't upended all your carefully laid house piles?"

"Sure, it's a process, merging your stuff together. And he's taken over my spare room with all his film equipment, although he and Double D are looking for an office in Seaside to set up shop, but it's okay. Does living with a guy scare you? Geez, Missy, you're not scared of anything."

"That's so far from the truth. What about those great whites you had me diving with?" The expedition a year ago to Guadalupe Island had had Grace deciding that freediving with the great whites was the best way to interact with them, eliminating the cumbersome scuba gear along with the noise it produced. It had become quickly apparent that Missy—while she had always loved being in the water with marine life, having done countless dives in her work with cephalopods—had nowhere near the brave factor that Grace possessed. And Missy had had to come to terms with that.

"You got past your fears and got back in the water," Grace said. "That's what counts."

"Thanks for the pep talk."

"Anytime. And maybe it was meant to be that you and Josh would end up in the Bahamas together. Take it as a sign from the universe."

Missy smiled. "Yeah. Okay. I'll talk to you soon."

"Let me know what happens with Brad."

"Will do. Bye."

Missy ended the call. She searched her bag for the one dress she'd brought with her—a simple pullover in hunter green that accented her eyes—pulled it on, slipped on some sandals, fluffed her hair, and put on a bit of makeup. Just eyeliner and a pat of powder to take the shine off her slight sunburn. Then she headed to the hotel restaurant to join the rest of the team for dinner.

Anticipation thrummed in her veins. It was for the night diving she would propose to the team, she told herself. But who was she kidding?

She looked forward to seeing Josh.

JOSH GLANCED at Missy across the table. She wore a dress that had him rethinking his choice of water with his fish dinner.

"We should do night dives," Missy said.

Everyone went silent.

Ken nodded almost immediately. "It's not a terrible idea."

Lucy frowned. "But we need water samples during daylight."

"Of course," Ken said. "But for the next few days, it would be a way to avoid the salvage team."

"And maybe they'll find what they're looking for and be done," Missy said, her voice subdued.

"True. All right, let me see what I can work out with the charter," Ken said. "If they agree, then we'll go out tomorrow night. Say eight p.m.?"

Everyone agreed. Since they'd already dived today, they'd need to wait twenty-four hours for safety reasons.

With the reprieve of not having to rise at the crack of dawn the following day, Josh ordered a beer when the waitress came back around. Everyone followed suit.

Once the drinks were in hand, Ken raised his and said, "To getting Benji deployed. Here's to a good week, everyone."

Several bottles tapped together in a toast.

Josh caught Missy's gaze, and it sure was nice to see some happiness on her face. He'd sorely missed it.

CHAPTER 8

Four years ago …

With the bottle of rum in hand—Brad had left it on the front windowsill of The Eight-Legged Mollusk—Missy followed Josh down a narrow trail to the secluded Tiki Hut Beach, anticipation thrumming in her veins. They'd caught the short ferry from North Bimini and were now back in South Bimini, but instead of returning to the Lab, he'd brought her here.

Josh was everything she imagined for a quick fling while in such a romantic setting as the Bahamas. Because it couldn't be any other way. Missy wouldn't let herself slide too far with him. She could handle her emotions as long as she went into the relationship with no expectations. Besides, Josh clearly wasn't a settling down type of guy.

Neither was Missy.

They got to the beach and Josh laid out the blanket he'd brought. It was a bit ratty, and the bright red and yellow design had faded, but at least it kept their butts off the sand. They sat side by side and Missy twisted the cap off the rum bottle. She offered it to Josh.

"Ladies first. It was your treasure hunt and you succeeded," he said. "You deserve to celebrate."

She took a quick gulp, letting the liquor burn her throat. She wasn't a fan of the hard stuff, but she needed it. She was nervous. About Josh. About wanting him. About worrying whether he really wanted her.

And why the hell should it matter? A hookup didn't require such deep thoughts. She was overthinking this.

She took another swallow of liquid courage.

The waves rolled in, their only demarcation the white froth as the water crashed down. Otherwise, the night was pitch black, lit only by a crescent moon.

"It makes you wonder about everything that's out there," he said, his gaze on the ocean.

A shiver went through Missy, partly from the light wind, but also the fear that the darkness and the inky depths kept hidden.

"I love it," she said. "And I'm also a smidge afraid of it."

"A little fear can be a healthy thing."

"Tell me a story about the Lab."

Josh paused, considering the request. "Well, this didn't happen on my watch, in fact it was likely many years ago, but there were a few photographers visiting the Lab and one of the managers suggested they capture a tiger shark, release it into a canal in South Bimini, and then 'wrangle' it for the cameras. And I know what you're thinking, it sounds terrible and unethical, so it's amazing how far we've come in such a short time in terms of protecting the rights of these fish."

Missy couldn't disagree. "I'm guessing it didn't go well."

"The release? I think it went okay," Josh said. "The plan was that the shark would leave the canal on its own during high tide, but it didn't and stayed around for another day. The following morning the staff was at the canal waiting for a pickup on a skiff when a very expensive looking speedboat pulled up to the dock. I should add that back then South Bimini was a major shipment hub for drugs passing between South America and the U.S. The men on board were straight out of a gangster movie, and one of them asked if a shark had been released in the canal, adding very angrily that his kids often swam there. Everyone was certain they were about to be shot. They quickly said they would never do it again, and thankfully the thugs sped away."

"And that's why humans are more frightening than sharks. Did the tiger eventually leave?"

"Yep."

Laughter filtered back to them.

Missy strained to see in the dark. "Are those people …."

"Skinny dipping. We need to go."

Suddenly, a spotlight illuminated the beach. "This is the police. Please come out of the water."

Josh grabbed Missy's hand, but they ran directly into another officer.

MISSY SLIPPED into bed as quietly as possible, having done the minimum bedtime routine—she'd quickly brushed her teeth and that was it—and glanced at her watch.

3:30 a.m.

It had been a long night.

"It must've been some date," Grace said into the darkness.

Missy flipped her pillow over, searching for the cold part. "Sorry to wake you. And it wasn't really a date." She tried to tamp down her frustration. Josh had flirted, at least Missy thought so, but it hadn't gone any further than that.

"Then why are you just coming back now? Did you go skinny dipping after all?"

Missy suppressed her frustration over the evening. She suspected that if she'd tried, Josh would have been able to ignore her nakedness, no problem.

"No," Missy said. "But we were caught up in a sting by the police. We were at the station for the last several hours."

"Really?" Grace laughed. "Sorry to hear it. Did you find the rum?"

"Yes."

"Well, that's something. Glad you're not in the slammer."

"Thanks."

"Good night, Missy."

"Night."

After that, the days became a routine of helping Grace in the early mornings testing her shark array on lemon sharks in the mangroves, afternoons on the charter boat that Billy had loaned her so that she could help Josh chase sharks in his Bat Suit, and nights working the late shift on the long lines for the Lab. The few spare hours she had, she worked on her own shark project.

She was exhausted, but she didn't want to give up any of the work, so she grabbed catnaps where she could. It was just as well since it didn't give her much energy to dwell over the fact that Josh hadn't made a move on her. Would he have if they hadn't been detained by the police that night on the beach? That had been a week ago. Josh had had plenty of chances for a romantic overture, but still ... nothing.

Missy was pretty sure he liked her. Occasionally there was heat in his eyes when she caught him looking at her. And she definitely liked *him*. Watching him in his wetsuit each day, all muscles and strength and masculine grace, had stoked her libido and she was considering that she would need to stop their daily excursions if he was never going to touch her. But then she chided herself for being petty, for letting lust cloud her work ethic, although she'd never worked harder than this past week, so ... a confusing paradox.

She had to concede there was precious little privacy at the Lab, so a relationship was hard to pursue, although somehow Grace and Brad kept theirs so low-key that more than once Missy wondered if they'd broken up. But mostly her time with Grace was spent talking about computer science and sharks, and Missy was fine with that. She really didn't want to know the details of Grace's love life with the person Missy tried her best to avoid most days.

When Brad had learned that Missy had found the rum bottle, he'd scoffed, saying he'd made it easy, so she'd have an easy go of it.

Gee thanks.

It was a balmy afternoon as she guided the boat along the coastline. Josh was in the water, following a tiger shark in his Bat Suit. They were in sync now and she could follow him easily, the water profile at the surface giving his presence away.

His tests were going well. The problem was finding sharks to chase. Sometimes the creatures would ditch him. And if they really put on the speed, he couldn't keep pace.

A flush of bubbles surfaced where Josh was cruising below. That wasn't normal. She frowned and cut the throttle.

For several long minutes, she scanned the area, wishing not for the first time they had radio contact with one another. But Josh was capable in the water, she reminded herself, and besides, if something were to happen, he could simply exit the cage and come to the surface.

But another two minutes passed, with more bubbles, and Missy's unease grew. What if Josh couldn't leave the cage for some reason?

She punched the anchor control and grabbed her scuba gear. She unspooled the winch and was in the water in less than thirty seconds, swimming toward the location of the bubbles with the winch hook in hand.

When she spotted the Bat Suit, it was deeper than Josh had ever taken it, her depth gauge showing sixty-three feet. He was still inside the cage, working the impeller, which kept stopping and starting. He caught sight of her as she neared, then suddenly the winch line went taut.

It wasn't long enough to reach him.

She tugged but there was no give. Her eyes met Josh's and he understood the issue. She could return to the boat and move it closer to him, then maybe the line would reach. She pointed upward but Josh shook his head.

She tapped two fingers onto the palm of her opposite hand. Josh responded to her request of how much air he had left with a chopping motion across his throat but then he added a hand signal: his thumb and forefinger two inches apart.

Okay. He had a little air left but not much.

He went back to trying to get the impeller to start, which whirred and then stopped. He kicked his feet to maintain his depth. He hadn't needed flippers while inside the cage but three days ago he'd decided to take them on his dives as a backup.

Missy estimated the distance between them. If she let go of the hook to reach him, it would float away, making it harder to get it back in hand. She reached down to her flipper and attached the hook into the strap, then she stretched forward.

Josh saw what she was doing and managed to get the impeller to run in spurts so he could turn to face her. After several starts and stops, she was finally able to grab the front of the cage. She pulled hard to bring it toward her, then she removed the hook from her flipper and attached it to one of the slats. Then she grabbed the spare air canister she'd attached to her dive vest and passed it to Josh. He removed his regulator and fit the mouthpiece of the canister into his mouth.

She gave a thumbs up, indicating she was going to ascend and start the winch. He responded also with a thumbs up. She kicked hard to ascend. The spare air would buy five minutes, tops.

Once at the boat, she quickly hoisted her scuba tank onto the back platform, and then her flippers. She grabbed the ladder and grunted as she dragged herself from the water. Pushing wet hair from her eyes, she hit the winch button and it began hauling up the Bat Suit.

She thought of jumping into the water to make sure there were no problems, but she resisted the impulse. Her father's words echoed in her head.

"Don't leave the boat. Especially in a rescue."

But she'd already disobeyed. *Sorry, Dad*. It had been necessary. However, doing so now would be foolhardy, except that panic welled in her chest. What if Josh died. A debate ran rampant in her mind over whether to jump back in the water, her stress building at the same rate as her ambivalence.

The winch stopped with a jerk.

Oh, shit.

She hit the on/off button—once, twice. Then a third time. The motor must have overloaded. She searched a cubby hole, found the winch handle, inserted it, and began to manually crank it. Fatigue set in swiftly. The cage was large, and she was fighting the current, but she refused to stop—Josh's life depended on it.

Finally, the cage popped up beside the boat. She set the winch to lock and leaned over the side to grasp one of the slats. Josh lifted his face and sucked in a breath, but there was precious little room between the top of the cage and the surface of the water.

"Are you out of air?" she yelled.

"Yes."

He struggled to keep his face out of the water. The ocean had become choppy, and the Bat Suit kept sinking below the surface.

She retrieved a grappling hook and grabbed the cage, hauling it closer to the boat, then she tried to open the door, but the latch was jammed. She quickly handed a snorkel to Josh, buying him more time.

She searched for a crowbar. Did they even have one? She couldn't remember ever seeing one but found a large screwdriver. Good enough. But jamming it into the latch mechanism proved difficult, the boat and the cage were bobbing too much.

"Give it to me," Josh sputtered, his head leaning back in his struggle for air.

Before she could think of all the reasons not to give the screwdriver to him, the least of which was that he might drop it and it would sink to the ocean floor, she completed the hand-off. He began jimmying the latch while Missy used the grappling hook to keep the cage near the boat.

Finally, the latch gave way and the door swung up. Missy leaned as far out of the boat as she could to help drag Josh out of the cage.

When they were both sitting on the boat at last—Josh on the

floor and Missy perched on one of the bench seats—they both didn't say anything as they struggled to catch their breaths.

"You're bleeding," Missy said, alarmed when she saw red all over his right hand. She retrieved the first aid kit, then stepped over him to kneel beside the injured hand and went to work cleaning it.

"It got caught on the cage there at the end."

"What happened?"

He hissed when she poured antiseptic on the gash just above his thumb.

"Sorry," she added.

"I lost power," he said. "I couldn't maintain the buoyancy and rolled, and the lock brushed against a rock and bent."

"I wondered why you didn't simply abandon the suit and ascend."

He released a frustrated breath. "I'm glad you found me."

She glanced up and caught his gaze. "Me too, but you weren't that deep."

"I managed to restart the motor and climb, but it kept cutting out. And then I started running out of air."

She tied off the gauze she'd wrapped around his hand. "You could have drowned, Josh. Is the Bat Suit worth it?"

"This cheap version?" he asked with a raised brow as he released a cynical laugh. "No. I need more money to build it right."

She repacked the medical supplies and shut the case. "So we're done with the suit." She remained where she was, squished against him at the back of the boat.

"You sound disappointed."

"It's my only chance to be alone with you."

He pinned her with a look that jolted her clear to her toes.

"Why haven't you kissed me?" she asked, throwing caution to the wind. Josh's near death had rattled her.

"Because you haven't asked," he replied, simple and matter-of-factly.

"Wait … that's what you've been waiting for?" She bounced into him as the boat rocked.

"Just because I want you doesn't mean I can have you."

She didn't bother to hide the incredulity building in her. "What are you talking about, McKittrick? I like you. I thought that's been obvious."

He broke eye contact and looked around the boat. "I'm not a fan of one-night stands."

That brought Missy up short. Not that she wanted only one night with him, but to be honest, she hadn't really thought much beyond the fact that she was slowly and steadily becoming crazy about him. It was almost an irritation. So maybe she did understand.

She leaned back. "Okay, I get it. Maybe we should just be friends." But her body and mind screamed no.

He brought his attention back to her, and it caused body parts to tingle and spark, preventing her from moving away from him.

"Is that what you want?" he asked.

She licked her dry lips. "No."

He moved his mouth close to hers. "Then I would like to kiss you."

She gave a tiny nod, anticipation swirling in her belly. The boat rocked again, and their foreheads knocked against each other.

"Ow." She covered half her face with her palm, while Josh winced.

As pain throbbed above her eye and she began to wonder if this wasn't meant to be, Josh used his free hand to clasp behind her neck and bring her lips to his. The kiss was firm and direct, the pressure from Josh's hand keeping her mouth immobile against his as the boat danced in the late afternoon chop. Finally, he lessened the contact slightly, and she responded to his hungry mouth in kind. He tasted salty, his skin cool from being wet, and she sought to warm him up with her lips and her hands, her fingers sliding into his damp hair.

Their position was awkward and with his injured hand it was difficult for him to touch her. She climbed onto his lap and straddled him, and the mouth plundering became mutual, his arms wrapping around her, causing Missy to shudder. She'd imagined being in his arms more times than she cared to admit this past week, and now that she was it didn't disappoint.

She wore only a t-shirt and khaki shorts, so Josh slipped his uninjured hand under both, exploring her backside and as much of her buttocks as he could reach before the waistband of her shorts stopped him.

Pressing against him released another delicious shudder from her lower body, but his wetsuit made it difficult to slide into a better position.

"You need to take this off," she said.

"Are you sure?"

She leaned back and met his gaze. "There's no privacy anywhere but this boat. If you want me, you can have me right now."

"Just for the record," he said, "there's not much privacy here either. Anyone could come upon us at any moment."

"C'mon, McKittrick." She smiled against his mouth. "Live a little."

He leaned forward slightly, and she helped him unzip the wetsuit down his back. His injured hand caused a bit of a slowdown as she had to carefully pull the neoprene over it without dragging the bandage with it, but soon she had him stripped down to a very revealing pair of speedos with a square leg, so there was a bit more coverage than the traditional skimpy swimwear, but not by much.

An enticing vee of hair led to those speedos, and she drank in the view of his muscular abs. She'd been enjoying his eye candy for the past week as he'd sometimes had the top of his wetsuit pulled down, but now she could finally indulge her desire to touch every inch of him.

And she did.

He soon had her completely naked and lying atop a towel on the floor of the boat. The space was narrow, bracketed on each side by bench seats, and it somewhat restricted their movements, but that seemed only to heighten the encounter.

He covered her body with his and the rocking of the boat

matched the joining of their bodies. Josh made love to her like he was branding her, and the intensity overtook Missy, making her desperate for him. The release was violent, catching her off guard, and she shook and shuddered with a pleasure that bordered on pain.

For a time, all they did was try to catch their breath as the ocean cradled them in the waves. Missy clung to Josh, refusing to let him go. But when the faint buzz of a boat motor could be heard in the distance, Josh pushed off her.

"Company?" she asked, immediately missing his heat. Her body felt limp, almost like liquid.

"They're moving away. We're good." He looked down at her, his gaze filled with intention and desire, and her body responded, wanting to welcome him back, wanting to entice him.

"I knew this would be a problem," he murmured.

She wasn't quite sure what he meant. She sighed and tussled her hair, enjoying the aftermath of the best sex of her life. "But it's a good problem. Right?"

"We should head back."

She reached out her hand. "Just a few more minutes."

He accepted her invitation. It was more than just a few minutes.

CHAPTER 9

Present Day

Missy entered the water first with her dive light on and hovered at the surface while the rest of the crew joined her. Her job was to keep everyone safe, so her attention would be split between watching the crew for any signs of distress—although they were also in buddy pairs as an extra backup—as well as keeping a check on the weather conditions. Thankfully the sky was clear and filled with stars against the black night sky, but there was a wind of ten knots out of the east, causing a bit of chop at the ocean surface and some stronger currents, which she could feel now that she was in the water.

Her dive buddy was Josh—assigned by Ken since the other crew members had specialties that kept them together. Josh moved beside her in full scuba gear, instead of the rebreather. Missy was also in the less cumbersome scuba since they wouldn't be going to the bottom tonight.

The plan was general mapping of the hole, as well as Andy and Lucy taking water samples. Ken and Sarah would be photographing the creatures they encountered. And Josh would be using an underwater drone to scout deeper. The apparatus was clipped to his buoyancy vest along with an underwater iPad to control the device.

It was the Bahamas so the water was warmer than elsewhere in the world, but it was early December, and they would be diving deep into the blue hole, so each of them had on a three-millimeter wetsuit.

There was no moon, which gave the stars more sparkle but left the ocean an inky and scarier place in Missy's mind. It was always a conundrum for her—she loved the ocean, she loved her work, but sometimes it crept into those places in her mind where she fought to keep her fears at bay, or at least buried until later when she could deal with them, preferably in the light of day, poolside.

Everyone was now in the water, and they formed a circle.

Ken's voice came over the radio system. "Everybody ready? Sound off."

"Sarah."

"Andy."

"Lucy."

"Josh."

"Missy."

Missy and Josh brought up the rear as everyone descended. In addition to her personal dive light, Missy had a larger one that she shined on the divers, lighting the surroundings.

They began on the shallow reef as they had previously. Josh had agreed to be the eyes in the back of her head, so she scanned a one-hundred-eighty-degree arc, mostly for sharks.

As they neared the edge of the sandy reef at around thirty feet, it dropped away to an abyss of blackness, and Missy had to make every effort to quell an impulse to swim back to the boat and get the hell out of the water.

Thanks, Grace, she thought to herself sarcastically. Diving with some of the biggest great whites on earth with Grace last year had given Missy a concrete picture of her nebulous ocean fears.

She thought of the deceased diver somewhere below them. Or

maybe he wasn't there anymore. Maybe the sharks had already taken care of him.

Neither thought made her feel better.

Get your head on straight, Rembert.

Ken led the group and began to descend along the inner wall of the hole. Feather duster worms waved in the water. As they moved deeper, several sharks darted in and out of the light. They looked like Caribbean reef sharks and seemed to have no interest in the divers, swimming away as soon as they could.

Missy's project at Bimini had been on apex shark predation, and although she had left the project after her dad had died, her advisor had completed it later, showing that in some reef ecosystems, Caribbean reef sharks didn't fill the role of top predator.

That meant there was usually another dominant species.

She focused into the depths, and then on impulse swam downward, pumping her flippers to get to Ken quickly.

"Ken, hold up," she said.

She came ahead of him so he could see her and held her hand up to get him to halt, which he did. She refocused her attention and shined her light into the inky depth. The Caribbean sharks had disappeared.

The bigger shark rose quickly, almost catching her off guard, but she was ready. She deflected the fish with a hard push on the snout as it swam directly at her, and then it veered off.

A bull shark. Maybe twelve or thirteen feet long. And a male, so he was possibly territorial.

"That's a big one!" Sarah proclaimed.

"Could there be another?" Lucy asked, worry evident in her voice.

"I don't think we should split up," Missy said. The plan had been for each team to collect their data separately to save time, but the bull had changed that. They didn't need the damned thing ambushing one of them.

Missy continued to scan beyond with her light. Josh joined her, helping to illuminate the area. "I think it's time for the drone," he said.

He unhooked the device, powered it up, and began a slow descent, watching the progress on the iPad. Everyone closed ranks more closely to keep watch.

They adhered to this routine for the next hour. The drone cleared the way before they followed. Luckily the bull shark didn't reappear, and Andy and Lucy were able to gather several water samples at various depths while Ken, Sarah, and Josh captured data on the layout of the hole.

Missy checked her depth gauge. They were at one hundred twenty-three feet, further than they should be in scuba, but they should be okay if they didn't go any deeper.

"Air check," Missy said.

All responded at half a tank.

They each had an extra tank, although it was to be used for the decompression stop if needed.

Missy checked her watch to make note of the time. "We've got ten minutes," she said. "Let's wrap this up."

"There's some interesting topography about fifteen feet beyond," Josh said. "Let's check it out."

"Roger that," Missy said.

They all followed Josh as he led them to the indicated spot. Vertical rock protrusions greeted them. Missy caught sight of octopus and eels, but being shy animals, they hid in their dens. Missy could well imagine how ominous they all looked in their scuba gear and bright lights, as well as Josh's underwater drone accompanying them.

There was a hole below them.

"Hold up," Josh said. "I want to send the drone down."

"I'm going to check out the perimeter of this promontory," Ken said.

"Five minutes," Missy said. "Don't be late."

"Roger," Ken said.

"We're going to do the same," Andy said, referring to him and Lucy.

"Roger," Missy replied. "Don't go further than fifteen feet."

Missy refocused on Josh, whose attention was wholly on his screen, watching the video feed from the drone. Suddenly it went blurry.

"Shit," Josh said. "The drone's stuck."

He spent a few long minutes trying to get the apparatus unstuck using the control panel on the iPad.

Finally he said, "I need to go down."

"Leave it," Missy said. "It's too dangerous."

"Agreed, but that drone is expensive equipment. At least let me see if it's within arm's reach. C'mon, Rembert, live a little."

She didn't miss the amusement in Josh's voice as he repeated words she'd used more than once with him.

"That phrase makes more sense topside," she said.

They were running out of down time. The longer they spent at this depth, the longer their decompression stop needed to be. It was her job to make sure they had enough air for every stage of the dive.

"Don't dawdle, McKittrick," she said, angling herself to watch Josh's descent. All she could see were his flippers as he went head-first into the hole.

A sudden strong current threatened to pull her down, and she fought against it.

"Talk to me," she said, not bothering to hide the mounting panic in her voice.

"I've almost got it." And then he blurted, "Sonofabitch!"

"What's wrong?"

"I think I just found Brad's body."

JUST BEFORE DAWN they returned to the hotel, and once again Missy found herself alone with Josh as they walked the outside hallway to their rooms.

"Shall we meet for breakfast?" she asked.

He glanced at her. "Why do I think you're suggesting we eat now."

"Well, it is almost five a.m., but I'm guessing the restaurant isn't open yet. But how about in an hour?"

"You're still an early riser?"

"We're already awake." She shrugged. "But I get it from my dad."

"The soul of a fisherman." He smiled. "Let me get showered and changed, and I'll meet you in an hour."

She'd reached her door. "See you then."

"See you, Rembert," he said as he kept walking, not looking back, his dark t-shirt stretched across his shoulders.

She'd always liked his physique, something deeply rooted in evolution, she supposed. His genes would complement hers if they ever had children.

And now she was thinking of having McKittrick's baby.

She fiddled with the bag that held her diving mask and other small items, delaying opening her door. A quick glance told her Josh's room was three doors down from hers. She went inside before he caught her looking.

Dropping the bag outside the bathroom, she stripped down and enjoyed a hot shower, trying not to imagine Josh doing the same three rooms away.

If she asked, would he give them another try? Is that what she wanted?

God, yes.

When had she decided she wanted a second chance? She couldn't pinpoint it exactly—it had simply creeped up on her in the last twenty-four hours. This wasn't real, she kept reminding herself. It was simply the same lust that had governed their relationship four years ago, leaving her overwhelmed and confused. It was the very reason she'd walked away from him back then. Things had been complicated with losing her dad so suddenly, and she'd had little confidence that their relationship back then was up to the challenge. So she'd cut the ties, clean and final, making it easier for everyone.

And now here she was, wanting to jump right back in.

What the hell did it mean?

Did she really have a right to ask? And maybe he was involved with someone, maybe seriously, maybe not so seriously, but either way he might no longer harbor any feelings for her beyond a vague heartache from when she'd left him four years ago.

By the time she was dressed and had dried her hair and pulled it into a ponytail, she'd managed to talk herself off the "Josh cliff."

She was being foolish. She'd made a choice then and she should stick by it. It wasn't fair to him to ask for more. They had to work together, and she never wanted to be that person who made it awkward.

She decided that she could be Josh's friend, and that she would try hard to be a good one. A good mensch. A good work partner. She at least owed him that.

She grabbed her purse that held her room key, lip balm, gum, and her cellphone, and left her room.

JOSH FOUND Missy sitting in a chair in the lobby, tan legs crossed, scrolling through something on her phone. She smiled when she saw him, and he experienced déjà vu, taking him back to their time in Bimini, when they were together, when he would've had every right to gather her in his arms and kiss her.

But he hadn't done that back then. They'd tried to keep their relationship on the down low. The Shark Lab was a small and tight knit community, and gossip spread like wildfire. Josh hadn't liked anyone knowing his business. It struck him then how much he'd tried to keep his relationship with Missy under wraps. Had he said as much to her? He must have. And she had agreed. Hadn't she?

Was that what pushed her away?

"Is the restaurant open?" he asked.

She stood. "Yes. Right at six. Your timing is good."

They made their way to the hostess, who let them sit wherever they wanted. The restaurant was mostly empty although there were a few hardy early birds.

"I think I'll hit the buffet," Missy said as she sat down, giving a nod for coffee when the waiter came by.

"Sounds good," Josh said. "I'll have the same."

"You can get your food whenever you like," the waiter said and left them.

Missy started to rise.

"Hang on," Josh said. "Can I ask you something?"

She sank back into her seat. "Sure."

"Back then .... Were you mad that I didn't want to advertise our relationship?"

"What? No."

"I probably didn't handle that well. I'm sorry."

"You're sorry?" She looked genuinely shocked. "Josh, I'm sorry. What I did was far worse. If I could go back, I'd do it differently."

He watched her, her expression a bit strained. "I suppose I'd do it differently too," he said quietly.

He thought he saw a flash of something in her gaze. A fire, a desire, but something held him back from crossing that line. Losing her had been the equivalent of drowning. No oxygen, no air, no breath. He'd been in a daze. It had completely blindsided him because he'd been unaware how deeply he'd fallen until she'd left him. Could he go through it again?

"This is complicated, Rembert," he said.

She licked her lips, drawing his attention to her mouth. Memories of those lips pushed past the dam he'd built against all things Missy. "You're right," she said, but the look in her eyes was open, searching. Did she want to try again?

His heartrate kicked up a notch. Wasn't this exactly what he'd always dreamed of? The return of Missy Rembert to his life, along with her begging to be let back in?

While he should've felt a bit smug that it had come to pass, instead he was filled with fear, not an emotion he usually let have free rein.

He'd never be able to let her go a second time. And he wasn't convinced she was here to stay. He supposed he'd felt it back then too but had instead chosen to ignore it. As much appeal as a fling with Missy Rembert in the Bahamas held, he couldn't let this get out of hand.

"Good."

"I think I'll get my food," she said.

He ignored the tinge of irritation in her voice as she stood and went to grab a plate. When she returned with eggs, potatoes, and two pancakes, she appeared to have shaken off her dour mood. They proceeded to have an amiable breakfast with both skirting the elephant in the room. Josh wasn't sure if he was happy about it or not.

As they were finishing up, Brad arrived with another man. Josh thought it was the one named Wyatt.

"Guess it's time to talk to Michaels," he said.

Missy tossed her napkin on the table. "I think I'll pass. I'll see you later."

She stood and left him.

Josh frowned. He had the impression she was mad at him, although he couldn't figure out why. He went to Brad's table, where he and Wyatt had just returned with plates loaded with food from the buffet.

"Just wanted to let you know we found a body," Josh said without preamble.

That caught both the men's attention.

"When?" Brad asked. "We never saw your crew yesterday."

Ignoring Brad's comment, Josh said, "The body is caught in an opening in a rocky area, along the north-northeast edge of the hole at a depth of one-hundred-twenty-three feet. We left a bright yellow bandanna tied off near the entrance."

"Thanks," Brad said. "We'll check it out. I guess I owe you a beer."

Don't overdo the gratitude, Brad. Rather than voice that sarcastic thought, Josh said, "There's something else I should tell you. About the Bat Suit."

"What are you talking about?"

"Look, I know you have a version of it here," Josh said. "And that it greatly resembles my design. So first off, you're welcome. Second, there's some issues you should know about."

"I didn't steal your design, Josh." Brad's refusal seemed to be more for his breakfast companion. "What we're using came from an engineer in Pensacola. We don't need any advice on how to run it. But thanks." Brad's dismissal was obvious.

Well, shit. Did he help the asshole or not?

Josh sighed and said, "The latching mechanism doesn't do well if it gets scraped or bumped against something. One time it jammed on me, and I barely made it out."

"Seems more like a diver problem."

"I also had issues with the impeller. The same one you have." And with that, Josh left them. He didn't feel like begging Michaels to see the light and be cautious. Maybe his teammate, Wyatt, would heed Josh's warnings. Either way, it was no longer his problem.

CHAPTER 10

Four years ago …

Missy stood in the mangroves with Grace, the saltwater coming to their knees. Grace held an old broomstick in the water, her sonar array attached at the bottom.

When a creature swam into the area, Missy wrote the information on a clipboard as Grace noted whether it was a shark or something else, and if it was a shark, then what genus. She also guessed the size and Missy clocked the time from her sport wristwatch. This would help correlate the data from the array.

Grace's goal was to increase the accuracy, and it had something to do with writing layers of computer code to help the array identify what was in the water, but as Missy had never been very good in the few computer science classes she'd been forced to take, she hadn't questioned Grace further. She was happy to take notes and help where she could.

"So Jen and some of the other interns are headed to Alice Town tonight," Grace said, without looking up from her surveillance of the water. "You want to go?"

"No. I'll pass."

"It's Josh, isn't it?"

Missy hadn't told anyone about her and Josh because … Josh hadn't told anyone. It had seemed simple enough. No one needed to know their business. But it had been three weeks now of them sneaking around, and it was beginning to wear on her. Not the part about being with him—he was by far the most intense relationship she'd had—but the part about not being able to talk about it.

Surely Grace was a safe bet to keep it to herself.

Missy cleared her throat. "Maybe."

"Lemon shark, about six feet," Grace said.

Missy looked at her watch and made the entry.

"I wondered," Grace murmured. "Because you two sure are careful."

"Then how did you suspect?"

Grace shrugged. "Josh just seems … different. Happier, if you must know."

The comment filled Missy with something akin to sunshine and rainbows.

"Sawfish," Grace said. "Four feet."

Missy added it to her notes.

"Well, don't worry," Grace continued. "I won't say anything."

Missy chewed on her lower lip. "You and Brad don't keep your relationship a secret. Should I be worried about Josh's secretiveness?"

Grace paused and lifted her gaze. "Well … I don't know. Josh has always been very private. I guess you should just ask him."

"Yeah, you're right." She'd bring it up tonight.

Grace's attention was diverted back to the water. "Aww," she crooned. "A baby lemon. I think it's only twelve inches long. Just the cutest thing ever."

Missy was convinced that if Grace could somehow live out here in the mangroves, no one at the Lab would ever see her again.

~

JOSH RETURNED from what seemed an endless day checking long lines and went straight to the showers. He and Missy were supposed to meet up after dinner out near the airport. They'd found some small palapas at the Bimini Sands Beach that were secluded, and there was usually no one there in the evenings.

After donning a clean t-shirt and khaki shorts, he went to the kitchen to grab a cup of coffee. No one was around and he resisted the urge to go to Missy's room just to say … hi. He had tried to keep his reaction to her from getting out. There were plenty of opinions amongst the Labbers when it came to Grace's relationship with Brad, and much of it wasn't good. Not that Josh cared what people thought of him, but he suspected that Missy might, so it was best if they didn't advertise what they had.

He wasn't sure what they had, truthfully, but he certainly thought of Missy nonstop, his days revolving around when he could be alone with her.

Grace appeared. "There you are," she said, her tone bordering on censure. "Why weren't you answering your radio today?"

"It broke."

"Then why didn't you come in?"

"It would've taken too long. You know that. The lines needed to be checked."

Some of the starch came out of her. "Yes, I know."

"What's wrong?"

She glanced around as if making sure they were alone. "Missy's gone."

"What do you mean?"

"She got a call before lunch. Her father's had a heart attack. She was able to get a flight out around one p.m., and she had to take it." Grace paused. "We tried to reach you. She wanted to see you."

From the intensity of Grace's expression, it was clear she knew about him and Missy. The weight of what she'd said hit him. Missy was gone. And he hadn't been here to offer support. To say goodbye.

An achy void filled his chest, making him feel as if he'd made a terrible mistake. "I'll call her."

"She's probably still traveling, so maybe wait until tomorrow."

CHAPTER 11

Present Day

As they approached the Blue Hole, the sun setting in a blaze of orange, Josh saw the other boat at the same time as everyone else.

"Sink or Swim is still here," Ken said, then he turned to the captain. "Park us on the opposite side. Who knows how long they'll be staying."

As the captain turned the boat to avoid the other team, the radio crackled. "It's Sink or Swim," the voice said. "We could use some help."

The captain grabbed his handset. "What's the trouble, over."

"We've got two men in the water we can't locate. Could use an assist."

"Roger that." The captain looked at Ken. "We have to help."

"Of course," Ken said.

The captain motored them across the blue hole.

As they came alongside the other boat, Josh asked the Sink or Swim crew, "What happened?"

"Brad and Wyatt went looking for the body based on your directions, but they were having trouble finding it. Then we lost radio contact. We've been looking for them, but so far nothing. Since you know the location of the body, could you find it again?"

Josh nodded.

"I'll go with you," Missy said.

They geared up and got in the water.

"Do you think you can find it?" Missy said over the radio.

"Yes." But Josh knew how easy it was to get disoriented down there. He hoped he could retrace his steps.

After descending for twenty minutes, frustration pushed at Josh. The rock formation was nowhere in sight. But then he felt the pull of the current, the same as they had the previous day. He made another circular sweep, Missy to his right, and he finally spotted the hole. A quick inspection showed the body to still be caught inside.

He scanned the area, his dive light a singular beam in the inky darkness. They were deep and it was dark, and it was unsettling.

"Where could they be?" Josh asked.

There was no sign that anyone had passed this way.

"This current," Missy murmured.

It wanted to pull them downward and away from the jutting rock, and they both were fighting against it to remain where they were.

"Are you thinking what I'm thinking?" Missy asked.

"That they got pulled in?" Josh replied. "Maybe."

"We should check it out."

"If they're stuck down there then we'd get stuck too. We need a rope."

They had to return to the boat, at which point they switched out their air tanks for new ones and made sure they each carried a backup. Ken and Sarah also got in the water with them as did two of the men from Sink or Swim. Missy had insisted she should investigate while Josh and the others held onto her with the rope. She was the lightest and the most qualified. Josh didn't like it, but she was right. The plan was that if she found them, she would attach a second rope to the men and then they would all be pulled out together.

They returned to the jutting rock formation where the pull of the current could be felt. Josh checked Missy's rope, assuring himself that it was tight. She gave a thumbs up and then disappeared below. Josh had the rope attached to him, and the rest of the team was behind him, attached in tandem. They should be able to hold themselves in the water column and reel Missy back.

"Status report," Josh said into his radio.

"Still descending," Missy replied. "Nothing yet, but the current is getting stronger. It's really pulling me down."

"Copy. Keep us posted."

She kept checking in for the next ten minutes, after which she exclaimed, "I see them. Shit."

"What?"

"One of them is in the Bat Suit. The other is outside, but they're both trapped against a small opening. There must be a tunnel that leads to the ocean and it's trying to suck them in."

Then she screamed, and Josh lost radio contact.

"Missy, come in. Missy!"

The rope went slack in his hands. *Fuck.*

"Let some rope out," he demanded into his headset. "I'm going down."

After being flung like a rag doll, Missy slammed into Brad's Bat Suit, the suction from the current so strong that she couldn't move.

"Brad, can you hear me?" she yelled. They made eye contact, but he shook his head.

He couldn't move, pinned on the far side of the cage. The other diver was pinned on the outside of the cage to her right. It looked like Wyatt.

This wasn't good.

"Josh, come in," she said.

Nothing.

She continued trying to reach anyone on the radio, but static was the only response. She reached for the rope that Josh had tethered to her, difficult with the current pushing so hard, but when she was finally able to grab it, a frayed end greeted her. Her heart sank. During her tumble it must have gotten caught on a rocky edge and snapped.

Missy looked at Brad again, but the bleak look in his eyes told her they must've been stuck for a while.

She went back to the radio, trying to hail anyone, but she got nothing.

Movement beyond the edge of her diving light coalesced into a diver coming toward her.

Josh.

Relief and an irrational surge of affection flooded her. He'd come for her. But then the current caught him, and he began spinning like she had, and he had no more control than she'd had. All she could do was watch helplessly, unable to assist.

He tumbled until he slammed against the cage, barely missing her.

"Josh, do you copy?" she asked.

"I copy," he said, his voice strained and his breathing heavy.

She glimpsed his face from the right side of her mask. "The current is too strong, and I've got no radio contact with Brad or Wyatt."

"Roger that. Ken? Sarah? Do you copy?"

There was no response.

"Something is blocking radio transmissions down here," she said.

"I'm roped," Josh said, "so we just have to get all of us hooked together, and then hope that Ken will start hauling us out."

"Brad is trapped in the Bat Suit."

"I don't know if Ken and the others will have the strength to haul out the suit."

"Then you should take Wyatt first," she said. "I'll stay with Brad. Then come back for us."

Josh didn't reply.

"Josh, do you copy?" she pressed.

"Yeah. I don't like any of these options."

"I know. But Brad and Wyatt are running out of air, although I don't know how much is remaining. I can't get a reading because of the current. I don't know how much time we have left."

Luckily Josh was between her and Wyatt, so he moved closer to the man.

"The rope is going taut," she said. "Grab him!"

Josh had a tether with a hook and somehow he managed to get it around a strap on Wyatt's chest, and then the two of them slowly began moving away from them. The current was strong, and the divers above probably weren't anchored in any way, so they would struggle to maintain their positions and not get sucked downward. But they must've figured it out because Josh and Wyatt drifted away, eventually swallowed up by the darkness.

Missy looked at Brad. His face reflected defeat. She almost felt bad for him, except for the fact that her life was now in danger because of him. She tried to see his air gauge, but it was turned away from her.

His eyes widened suddenly, and it was clear he was beginning to feel the strain of his air running out. She had a second tank with its own regulator, but she needed to get closer to him so he could access it. Of course, he would need to remove his full-face mask. She didn't have a spare mask, but maybe he did. If not, his eyes and face would be unprotected in the cold, dark water, but at least he would be breathing. Her safety diving instruction had stressed remaining calm and dealing with one problem at a time. Easier said than done, with anxiety swirling in her abdomen, but it was her job to remain coolheaded.

She began moving in incremental inches toward the top of the cage. Brad watched her with mounting fear reflected in his eyes. When she finally reached a position almost above him—it felt like it had taken too long, but in truth she didn't know how much time had passed—she struggled to grab the extra regulator and get it passed through the cage slats. Thankfully Brad seemed to understand what she was trying to do, but when she almost had the task completed, she was blasted off the cage.

In a disorienting jumble, she flipped head over feet. Her mind registered two things—the current had obviously reversed, abruptly, giving them a window of escape; and she really needed to get Brad out of that cage.

When her momentum slowed, she took a few steadying breaths, forcing a calm and steady rhythm, ignoring the waves of nausea and dizziness. She had air, but Brad was perilously close to the end. And who knew how long the reverse current would last.

She cast her diver light in a circle around her, searching for him.

There he was, about twenty feet away, but distance could be misleading when there were precious few spatial references. She pumped her legs and got to him as fast as she could, pulling the knife from the sheaf along her leg. She hadn't attempted it earlier because she doubted she could have reached it against the current.

The Bat Suit was starting to sink so Missy grabbed it with a gloved hand. Brad was still conscious thankfully, so she jammed the knife into the latching mechanism, the same as she'd done for Josh four years ago. Back then it had been a screwdriver and it had worked, so the knife should be strong enough. As they began to sink, she worked it against the compressed latching mechanism, trying to leverage it. She shoved hard, and the cage finally opened. Reaching inside, she caught a hold of a strap on Brad's wetsuit, yanking him out as the cage sank into the black abyss below them.

For a moment, she struggled to keep them steady at their depth with the vortex the cage created pulling them downward. And then she realized that Brad had gone slack, unmoving.

Shit! She couldn't switch out his mask and regulator by herself without drowning him in the process, and he wouldn't survive the ascent to the surface. It would take too long.

A bump from behind startled her. Josh. She immediately brought Brad between them. Luckily Josh knew what she wanted to do when he presented an additional mask. He took Brad into his embrace to steady him, while Missy grabbed the extra regulator. She hesitated only a moment before lifting the bottom of his face mask and shoving the regulator into his mouth, praying that he didn't ingest too much water. She immediately pinched his nose. Josh pulled Brad's mask free.

Breathe, Brad. Breathe.

His body jerked, and his eyes flew open, his chest moving. It wasn't perfect, but he was getting air at least. She grabbed the spare mask and pulled it onto Brad's face. He nodded and cleared the water himself, looking stressed but at least he was alive. She took one of Brad's arms and Josh took the other, and together they helped him ascend to the remaining team, and then finally to the surface.

CHAPTER 12

Four years ago …
San Francisco

Missy glanced at her cellphone. Another text message.

> GRACE: I'm so sorry about your dad. I've been there and I know how you feel. Josh is worried about you. You should call him when you feel up to it.

Missy took a deep breath and put her phone on silent, feeling anew the unsteadiness of every moment of every day since her father had passed away. She'd returned from Bimini six days ago, requiring twelve hours of travel and feeling desperately lost the entire time. She'd made it to the hospital twenty minutes before her father had died—he'd been unresponsive and all she could do was hold his hand—and had been in a fog ever since.

What little energy she'd been able to muster each day had to be directed toward helping her mother sort out the details of a funeral and the myriad of paperwork that had ensued. And through it all, Missy had been fiercely missing the most important man in her life —her father.

When was the last time she'd spoken to him? It broke her heart that she couldn't remember.

"Are you ready?" The question came from a kind-hearted woman at the church. Missy couldn't recall her name, so she simply nodded.

Missy went to her mother and helped her stand, struck by how fragile the woman felt in her arms. Together they walked into the church.

George Rembert had been only forty-five years old, and for twenty-five of those years, he'd been the devoted husband to Missy's mother, Peggy.

Missy closed her eyes, willing the white-hot pain to a manageable place so she could help her mother through the most awful day of her life—saying goodbye to the love of her life.

LATER THAT NIGHT, when family and friends had finally left Missy and her mom alone in the small house where she'd grown up, Missy went to her childhood room.

Exhaustion swamped her, but she wanted to get this over with because she had no energy to deal with anything other than her mother and her grief. Tomorrow her only goal would be to get up and make her mother eat something for breakfast. And then she would deal with the next hour after that. And so on.

She didn't want to think about school or work. Or Josh.

He had left her voice messages. And he'd sent texts. They had all been kind.

But she couldn't feel anything anymore. And she was glad for it. The grief of losing her dad had been a blistering thing, and she'd been burned to nothing in the past week. But this afternoon, it had finally stopped, and thank God for it. Never mind that she was as numb as if her entire body had been injected with lidocaine. She was just relieved to be free of it.

She hit Josh's contact in her phone.

"Hello," he answered on the first ring. "Missy. How are you?"

"Hanging in there." She didn't recognize her voice. It sounded distant, almost detached from her.

"I've been trying to call you. I'm sorry I didn't get to say goodbye before you left."

"It's no problem."

"I can come there," he said, his voice oddly ... tender. In the short time Missy had known Josh, she never would have described him as emotional.

"No, it's okay."

He cleared his throat. "When do you think you'll come back to Shark Lab?"

The sooner she got this done, the easier it would be for them both. "Look, I'm not coming back. And you and I had fun, but we know it was never going to be long term. So no worries, you have no obligation to me. You take care, okay? 'Bye."

She ended the call before he could say anything, ignoring the wave of panic that shuddered through her, and took a deep steadying breath, wiping at the tears that had fallen down her cheeks.

No more dwelling on it.

Her father was gone. Learning to live without him was going to take every ounce of strength she possessed. What she and Josh had was so new, so fragile, that there was no way it would ever have survived the long journey she had ahead of her.

She had done Josh a favor by cutting him loose.

CHAPTER 13

Present Day

Josh had helped Ken and Andy deposit the gear in the hotel storage room while Sarah and Lucy had made sure Missy made it back to her room. It was after ten p.m. when they were finished. After the lengthy rescue of Brad and Wyatt, everyone had agreed they didn't have the stamina to continue working through the night.

"We'll regroup in the morning," Ken said.

"Sounds good," Josh replied, waving to the two men as he headed to his room.

But he never intended to go that far, instead stopping outside Missy's door. He didn't hesitate before knocking.

For a long moment, there was no response, and he thought maybe she was already asleep. Then the door opened, and Missy stood before him, wrapped in a towel, her hair wet. She must have just gotten out of the shower. He supposed he should've stopped to think about what he wanted to say exactly, to maybe have rehearsed it, but the truth was he hadn't had the patience.

"I need to talk to you," he said.

She stepped back and let him enter. When she shut the door he turned back to her, stopping her in the entryway.

"I made a mistake four years ago," he said. "I let you walk away from me, because I thought it was the right thing to do. When you finally called me back, I was prepared to fly to San Francisco the next day. I wanted to see you that bad." His voice broke. "And I'd wanted to be there for you. But then you ended it and ...." He ran a hand through his hair. "And I wanted like hell to argue with you, to tell you to give us a chance, but I knew you were in unimaginable pain, and I had no right to be so selfish." He cleared his throat as it threatened to close up, unshed tears pushing against his eyes. "So I let you go, and it was the single biggest mistake of my life. And in the time since then, I managed to convince myself that you really hadn't been that big of a deal to me, but that's simply not true. And tonight, having to leave you down there with Brad ... well, shit. I realized that I might've lost you again, only this time it would've been permanently. Maybe you don't love me, maybe you never did, but I love you, Missy. I did then, and I do now."

Missy watched him with wide eyes while he confessed, unmoving, but when he finally took a breath, she stepped forward and kissed him. Hard. Hungry. The fierce desire she ignited was accompanied by a relief so strong his knees nearly buckled.

He brought his arms around her, crushing her against him, deepening the kiss. Her lips parted and he devoured what she offered, his mouth slanting across hers and their tongues tangling.

Her towel dropped and his hands relearned every soft, sexy inch of her, to the dip of her buttocks and then everything below it. He lifted her up, and she wrapped her legs around him, and he carried her to the bed, laying her on it. She clawed at his t-shirt, and he helped her pull it over his head, tossing it aside. Then he unbuttoned his shorts, kicked off his shoes, and pushed away what remained of his clothing in one motion.

She pulled him to her, and he took her mouth again, relentless and desperate. He was hard and ready, and she was just as feral, lifting her body to his. He entered her in one complete thrust, then he paused, not wanting it to go so fast, but in truth he only had a second or two. He raised his head and looked into her eyes.

She released a shaky breath, then angled her body against his, increasing the pressure and the tension. So much for drawing it out. He thrust into her, every motion building his need, every motion a stark reminder of how much he'd missed her, of how effortless the chemistry had always been between them, of how she completed something in him that no woman ever had. As her cries signaled her release, he finally let himself go, falling into the deep blue with her.

MISSY RESTED her head on Josh's chest, her naked body partially covering his, comforted by the steady beat of his heart.

"This is such a treat," she murmured.

His hand was keeping her left buttock warm. "What's that?"

"Sex in a bed."

He laughed, the sound a low rumble in his chest. "I made some mistakes back then," he said. "One of which was never getting us a proper place to be together."

"It's all right. I didn't mind. Really. And if my dad hadn't ... well, if things had been different, I think I would never have walked away." Then she whispered, "I was so stupid back then. I needed the pain to go away, and anything else I felt went right along with it." She raised her head and looked at him. "I'm sorry."

His gaze reflected compassion. "I know."

"Do you mean it?" she asked.

"What?"

"Do you really love me?" God help her, but when he'd said it, something primal had been unleashed in her. Words she'd had no idea she needed. From him. Always from him.

"I think it hit me when I came back to the Lab that day and you were already gone. And then here when I saw you in the van. You looked so goddamned good. It was the luckiest day of my life."

She smiled. "Really?"

"Well, I wasn't thinking that then. I was thinking that I was over you, that I could absolutely work with you, and it wouldn't be a problem."

She shifted and fit her body on top of his, her breasts against his chest and her legs between his, and she brought her face to his. "I thought the same thing." She kissed him. When he grew hard against her, desire stirred anew, and she dragged herself up a bit to create some delicious friction between them.

He ran his palms up and down her back.

"I was wrong," she continued. "I'm glad I was wrong."

He cupped her buttocks and pulled her toward him so he could have access to her breasts with his mouth.

"Josh." She forced her face before his again. "I love you, too."

"You don't have to say it. It's okay."

"I know. But I do. I was a coward four years ago. I'm sorry I didn't give us a chance."

He grasped her hips and shifted her slightly so he could slide inside, pleasure rippling through her.

He brought his hands to her face. "You're not a coward, Missy. I didn't give you a lot to hang your hat on. I won't ever make that mistake again."

She felt him twitch inside her, and she laughed softly. "Hang my hat on, huh?"

"It's just a figure of speech."

He kissed her and she enjoyed controlling the rhythm as she let Josh McKittrick fill not only her senses, but her heart as well.

CHAPTER 14

San Francisco
Two weeks later

Josh draped an arm on Missy's chair as Grace described Missy's willingness to get back in the water with great white sharks after initially losing her nerve. It was early evening, and the setting sun left a warm glow through the window of the seafood restaurant.

"I knew I'd get you back in the water with sharks after you left Shark Lab," Grace said, taking a sip of her water, then smiling as the waitress brought her a mango margarita.

"I would've happily faced lemon sharks," Missy said. Then she turned to Josh. "You can't believe the size of the whites at Guadalupe Island. No normal person is excited to get in the water with them."

"Grace is no normal person," Alec Galloway said from where he sat across from Josh. "I thought you knew that by now." He took a sip of his beer.

Josh liked Galloway, mostly because he appeared to understand Grace's quirks, something Brad had seemed oblivious to. And if the glimmer on Grace's face was any indication, her affection for

Galloway ran just as deep. She had certainly never looked at Brad that way.

"So fill us in on what happened at the Blue Hole," Grace said.

"Well, after Brad's rescue, his team decided to call it quits," Missy replied. "Apparently, they told Howie Barrett's family that his body wasn't retrievable."

"And we all agreed with that assessment," Josh said.

"That was a strong current," Alec said. "Definitely something to take care around."

"We avoided the area after that," Josh said. "We spent the rest of the week gathering samples and then retrieving my benthic lander."

"And I want to talk to you more about that," Grace said, "but not here since I'm sure it will bore Alec and Missy. I'd like to look at your code. Did Brad get his Bat Suit back?"

"No," Missy said. "It was damaged, so they abandoned it."

"If you want to work on it again," Alec said to Josh, "let me know. I'd be happy to help."

Grace smiled with obvious pride. "Alec is pretty mechanical."

"We could get it patented too," Alec added. "It would be nice to put a little fear into Brad. I'm sure he's already in the process of stealing something from someone else."

The edge in Alec's voice caught Josh's attention. "You sound as if you know him," Josh said.

"I do. We surfed competitively when we were young, and he hasn't changed much. He almost cost me my job with Grace."

"But you were determined," Grace replied.

He looked at her. "I've always had to be determined when it comes to you."

Josh decided that if Alec were smart—and he was pretty sure the filmmaker was—then he'd be proposing to Grace any day now. Just as Josh was determined to do with Missy. But first things first. After spending the remainder of their time in the Bahamas together—either diving or locked in her hotel room—he'd gotten his ass out here to San Francisco as fast as he could once he'd returned to Houston. He hadn't come to her four years ago when her father had died. He wasn't making that mistake again.

After a hot and heavy afternoon in her apartment upon his arrival, they'd had dinner with Missy's mother, and the woman had given a clear stamp of approval, hugging Josh like he was already a part of the family. Frankly, it had humbled him.

And then Grace had driven up from Monterey with Alec, not giving them any down time. While Josh had been happy to catch up, it was also clear Grace was in her own version of mother-mode. There were subtle signs of scrutiny from her, but she soon settled into an accepting demeanor.

Missy had been very excited for all of them to get together, and it was obvious she considered Grace and Alec good friends, so he felt heartened that she so readily wanted to include him in the important parts of her life. It gave him hope that she was willing to give them a chance again. He'd already begun thinking about how he could transfer to a lab in northern California, but he would wait to tell Missy once he had the details ironed out.

The waitress brought out a charcuterie board and placed it at the center of the table.

"What are you both planning for Christmas?" Missy asked.

Grace transferred cheese and olives to her plate. "We're headed to Hawai'i next week."

"My folks are gathering all the kids together," Alec said.

Missy snatched a bunch of grapes. "Sounds fun."

"Are you kidding?" Grace's eyes went wide. "They'll be surfing Pipe every day."

"Only if the waves are there," Alec said. "We'll get to meet Brynn's new boyfriend. She's my little sister," Alec offered for Josh. "She hooked up with some physicist a few months ago in Bolivia, so she's bringing him for the big family meet and greet."

"You'll behave, right?" Grace asked.

"Absolutely not. If he can't put up with me and Tyler, then he doesn't deserve her."

Grace wrinkled her nose at him then turned to Missy. "What about you two?"

"Josh can stay for a few more days, then he needs to head back to work. But I'll be meeting him in Arizona the day after Christmas."

"What's in Arizona?" Alec asked.

"My folks," Josh replied. "And my brother."

Grace's eyebrows shot up and she stared at Missy. "You're going home to meet Josh's family?"

Missy narrowed her eyes. "Yes. Why?"

Grace laughed. "Congratulations, Josh. She's all yours."

He liked the admission.

Missy shook her head in a mock scowl as Grace added, "She's *never* met any parents. She's always had every excuse in the book. I knew you two were meant for each other. It sure took you both long enough."

Josh draped an arm around Missy's chair. "I agree," he said, "but now it's time to live a little."

Missy grinned at him. "It's time to live *a lot*."

Learn how Grace and Alec met in the full-length novel DEEP BLUE. She swims with great white sharks, and he will film it.

Catch up with Jen Fairfield and her romantic troubles with Dr. Gabe O'Grady in the short adventure SHARK REEF. A friends-to-lovers romance set in New Zealand alongside the wildest great white sharks on the planet.

Keep reading for a brand new Deep Blue short adventure!

Deep Blue Hawai'i

Dr. Grace Mann and her boyfriend, underwater filmmaker Alec Galloway, are in the Aloha State for a Galloway family Christmas. While surfing Pipe is on the agenda for the boys, Grace finds a way to get in the water with tiger sharks, but can Alec convince her to stay on dry land long enough for an important question?

While you can enjoy this story on its own, here is the reading order for maximum enjoyment.

Deep Blue (novel)
Deep Blue Australia
Deep Blue Réunion Island
Deep Blue Cocos Island
(these three short adventures are available in one collection: The Pathway Short Adventure Collection)
Deep Blue Hawai'i

DEEP BLUE HAWAI'I

Hawai'i
O'ahu, North Shore
December 23

Alec stopped the truck in the driveway of the home his parents owned near Waimea Point. The modest oceanfront house had four bedrooms and a great view. He hopped out, as did his brother, Tyler, and his sister's new boyfriend, Tristan Magee.

"I thought you said you could surf, Magee," Tyler was saying as they each pulled a surfboard from the bed of the truck and carried it to the garage. Alec wanted to wax them before they went out again tomorrow.

"I may have overstated my abilities," Tristan said.

"Okay," Tyler continued, "so what's the payment for not telling Brynn that you choked like a gremmie?"

"I did not choke." Tristan placed the surfboard he'd borrowed on the rack. "You didn't tell me we were going to Pipe. I'm not a professional. And what the hell is a gremmie?"

Tyler smiled. "Just a term for an inexperienced surfer. Next time we'll make sure you have baby waves."

Tristan removed his sunglasses, looking wiped. He'd eaten wave after wave, but Alec had to give him credit—he was persistent in his inexperience. "I'll buy a case of beer," Tristan said.

Alec laughed. "For each of us."

Magee swore under his breath as they entered the house through a side door, each of them kicking off sand-covered shoes. Alec's dad sat at the breakfast bar typing on his computer, wearing a rash guard and his swimming trunks.

"You planning on going out?" Alec asked him, surprised. They'd invited him but at the last minute he'd had to deal with business back in the mainland. He ran a consulting software company and had tried more than once to get Alec's girlfriend, Grace, to work for him, but her love of marine life tended to outweigh her computer science background.

"I figure if I stay in my surf gear," Jim said, "then I'll be able to sneak out quicker before the office or your mother knows."

Brynn came in from the back deck holding a cup of coffee.

"How was it?" she asked, her brown hair in a loose bun and still wearing the t-shirt and shorts she'd slept in.

"Magee's a natural," Ty said, the lie rolling off his tongue as he grabbed a banana from a basket on the breakfast bar.

"Really?" Brynn's expression brightened. "It went well?" She went to Magee and gave him a kiss.

Alec didn't miss the man's hand sliding down to his sister's butt. Some things a brother was better off not witnessing, although he had to admit that his little sister looked happy with this one. Magee had better not hurt her.

"Your brothers are trying to kill me," Tristan said.

"Only a little," Alec acknowledged.

Brynn looked at Magee more closely. "You look beat and it's only nine a.m. How many waves chewed you up?"

"What makes you think that?" Tristan released her but then sank to the couch, pulling her down with him. "Hey, Alec. Toss me a banana."

Brynn turned the full force of her attention to Tyler, and then to Alec. "You took him to Pipe, didn't you? He's not *that* good."

Alec ignored her and lobbed the fruit, which Magee caught with one hand.

"That's not what he said," Tyler said.

She turned to Tristan. "I'll take you surfing, baby." Then she swept her gaze over Alec and Tyler, a hard glint in her eyes. "My brothers are toast."

Tyler ignored her and instead asked, "Where's Lindsey?"

If Alec had to guess, Tyler's girlfriend—a professional mountaineer like his brother—was off hiking since she was just as restless as Ty at times.

"She went with Grace," his dad replied, rising from his seat and pouring himself another cup of coffee.

"To where?" Alec asked.

"She got a call about a dive, or something," Brynn cut in. "She tried to text you. Don't you ever check your phone?"

Alec hadn't. He'd been having too much fun surfing. And watching Tristan get tossed around. He found his backpack and fished out his phone. He quickly got caught up on the messages Grace had left him. *What in the hell?*

"I gotta go," he said.

"To where?" Ty asked.

"Grace is diving with tiger sharks with the intention of getting them to attack her." Alec grabbed the truck keys.

"I'll come with you," Ty said as he snatched a granola bar from a box near the microwave and a bottle of apple juice from the fridge.

"You boys better be back by three," his dad yelled after them. "Your mother has an early dinner planned."

As Alec drove, he tried to reach Grace, but it went to voice mail. He didn't leave a message and cut the call. He pulled up to the dock, grabbed his bag of diving gear from the back of the truck, and went to the Hanalei Dive Shop, Tyler keeping pace with him.

"Hey, Ronnie," Alec said, the door jingling as he entered. "I need a boat and some tanks. Can you hook me up?"

"Right now?" Ronnie said, wearing a colorful blue shirt to give the customers a taste of Hawai'i.

"Yeah."

Ronnie scanned his back room. "Okay," he said. "Give me a minute."

Thirty minutes later Alec was manning a small outboard, Tyler beside him, to a location that Ronnie guessed might be where Craig Welch, who was heading the controversial experiment, might have gone. A boat in the distance beckoned, and Alec went toward it, Tyler scouting with binoculars.

"It's our boat," Tyler said as they got closer. "I can see Lindsey."

An orange flag was flying, which meant divers were in the water, so Alec cut the throttle.

He began scanning to make sure he didn't accidentally run over someone who might be surfacing.

"Wait a minute." Ty's voice sounded ominous.

"What's wrong?" Alec asked.

"There's someone else on deck with Linds, and it looks like Stacy so-and-so."

Alec frowned. "Stacy Finnegan?"

"Yep. Your ex-girlfriend. Why would she be out with Grace?"

"How the hell should I know? I haven't seen Stacy in over three years." And he'd just as soon skip having to talk to her, but he wasn't leaving without Grace.

He brought them beside the other boat. When Lindsey saw them, she smiled and waved. Unfortunately, Stacy also saw them, and Alec knew the moment his ex realized it was him. Her body became rigid, and her face took on the scowl that had been present more often than not at the end of their relationship.

Lindsey came to the gunwale and grabbed the rope Ty threw at her, tying it off so the boats would remain side-by-side.

"Hey," Lindsey said. "How'd you find us?"

"Alec tracked you down."

"Where's Grace?" Alec asked.

"She's in the water," Lindsey said.

Stacy approached. "Small world, Alec."

"I guess so," Alec said.

"Do you two know each other?" Lindsey asked.

Ty coaxed Lindsey into their boat. "They used to date."

"Really?" Lindsey climbed over the two bobbing sides, and Tyler wrapped her in his arms and gave her a kiss, her blonde hair tumbling from its scrunchy and down her back.

"You're dating a Galloway?" Stacy said when he saw their affectionate greeting.

Lindsey smiled over her shoulder. "Is that a problem?"

Ty couldn't contain the glee in his voice as he said, "Oh, it gets worse, Stacy."

Tyler had never liked the woman. At the time, it had annoyed Alec, but now he had to concede that his brother had probably been right about her.

"Grace Mann is Alec's girlfriend," Ty added.

Stacy's surprise was genuine. "Really?" She shook her head and turned away.

Alec grabbed his gear bag and tossed it to the other boat. He jumped over and then turned back to Tyler. "Hand me the tanks." His brother lifted them over one by one.

"You're seriously going in the water?" Ty said.

"Damn straight."

Alec moved to the back of Craig's boat and started stripping down. Stacy frowned at him. The only other person present was the captain, and he seemed immersed in watching something on his phone, ignoring them.

"Better turn away if you don't want to see more of me," Alec said.

"It's nothing I haven't already seen. Of all the places I expected to run into you, it wasn't here."

"My folks vacation in Hawai'i every Christmas. You knew that." He pulled off his t-shirt and shorts and pulled on his wetsuit.

"Yes, of course," she said. "It's all coming back to me now, how you never invited me."

She wasn't wrong about that. The truth was, even then Alec knew she wasn't a long-term relationship. And he didn't bring those home to his mother.

"Why is Grace in the water trying to get tigers to bite her?" he asked.

"If you must know, she wasn't my first choice. Craig Welch designed a chain mail suit that he's hoping is impervious to shark bites. He needed to test it, but our first diver has food poisoning. He knew Grace and heard she was staying at the North Shore, so he called her. She jumped at the chance."

Alec didn't doubt that. If Alec had any competition for Grace's affection, he had no illusions that it was a shark. Any shark.

"Why aren't *you* in the chain mail?" he asked, checking his regulator.

"I'm too tall for the suit. And besides, I'm here to film it."

He pulled the tanks onto his back and grabbed his mask. "You're getting a lot of footage from here on the boat," he said, not bothering to hide his sarcasm.

"My camera jammed. I'm here to get my back-up."

Her comment reminded him of the tone of their relationship—they'd met on a dive in South Africa, both up-and-coming underwater photographers. At first, their shared interest along with the close quarters of diving every day had sparked a whirlwind romance that they'd managed to stretch into a year. But Stacy's drive to find work and desire to be recognized as at the top of her game had driven a wedge between them. Alec knew she'd never considered him her equal.

When she'd finally tromped all over his professional connections to get ahead, he'd been contemplating breaking up with her for at least a month. They had hardly been together during the last few months anyway, each of them working on separate jobs. Her final betrayal had only made it easier to end it over the phone.

It had honestly taken Alec one day to purge himself of any remorse or sadness over the end of their coupledom. The fact that her presence didn't trigger any type of affection—even of friendship—had him wondering what had been in his head when he'd been with her. It paled in every way to his relationship with Grace.

"Where are they?" he asked, trying not to imagine what might be happening to Grace at this minute.

She pointed to the east. "About a quarter mile that way. It's nice to see you again, Alec."

Perched on the gunwale, he fell backward into the water and went to find Grace.

~

GRACE READIED herself as the tiger shark approached. It was a smaller one, maybe only eight feet, but it had been the most curious of the three that Craig and his assistant, Joel, had been able to lure close with a bait box.

Early attempts to get the shark to latch onto her arm by simply shoving herself in front of the bait had failed, so now she held a piece of fish in her left hand while she blocked her body with her right arm.

The tiger took the bribe, coming close, and this time Grace got her arm in the fish's mouth. It clamped down before it realized that her limb was encased in a chain mesh suit and wasn't the meal it had been hoping for.

The shark shook her, its jaws exerting an uncomfortable pressure on her arm, and then it was over.

With her heart racing, she sought to steady her breathing, and then she inspected herself. No damage, and she hadn't even felt the sharp teeth against her skin.

Success! She grinned and gave a thumbs up to Craig and Joel.

From the depths, a larger shadow materialized, and she quickly set herself up again, still holding the fish bait from the other encounter. She braced herself as this tiger, probably a twelve-footer, came in fast.

She didn't have time to offer her forearm as a tasty chew toy. Instead, the shark rammed her, and both of her arms got caught in the wide mouth. Shaking her like a rag doll, all she could do was hang on and pray her arms didn't break.

Suddenly another diver appeared, shoving hard at the shark's snout. It released her and swam off. She stretched out her arms, and thankfully both worked. She was a bit sore, but like before the shark's teeth hadn't penetrated the chain mail.

When she made eye contact with the diver, she was surprised to see Alec staring back at her, stress lines marring his forehead. He wasn't happy.

She supposed it had looked worse than it was. Giving a thumbs up, she smiled around her regulator. He must've gotten her messages.

Craig signaled they should ascend. The camera woman—what was her name? Sarah? Stacy?—wasn't around. Had she missed filming the entire encounter? Grace's annoyance grew as they headed back to the boat.

GRACE REMOVED her regulator at the surface. "How'd you find me?" she asked Alec who was beside her.

"I've got connections at the dock," he said. "I wish you would've waited for me. Can I just add that watching that tiger clamp onto you just shaved a few years off my life?"

"It was fine. Really," she added. "The suit worked like a charm." Except that she was having trouble treading water while wearing the heavy chain mail, her muscles starting to fatigue. "But I need to get out."

Alec swam to the boat, and along with Craig and Joel, they hauled her out of the water. Alec sat beside her on the swimming deck and helped to pull off her tank, then it took several minutes to get her out of the chain mail.

"How did it feel?" Craig asked her.

"A little like a rag doll."

"Any injury?"

Alec scowled at that comment, inspecting her arms now that the suit was gone. Red marks were visible, and she guessed they'd turn into some nasty bruises.

"You did great, Grace," Craig said. "Thank you so much." Then he looked at Alec.

"Oh, sorry," Grace said. "This is Alec Galloway."

"The filmmaker. Stacy has mentioned you."

That was her name—Stacy. And she knew Alec?

Alec stood, helping Grace to her feet, and they went to the interior of the boat to sit on a bench.

"Did anyone film the encounter?" Grace asked, noticing the woman at the front of the boat, essentially avoiding everyone.

"No," Joel said, irritation clear in his voice. "Can you come out again tomorrow?" he asked her.

"Sure. Hey, maybe Alec could film it?" She looked at him with hope in her eyes, offering a smile to placate the concern in his gaze.

"I'd rather just keep my eye on you if it's all the same," he said quietly, for her ears only. Then he stood and started moving his gear to the boat he'd tethered to this one.

Lindsey sat beside Grace. "Did you hear?"

Grace frowned. "Hear what?"

"Alec and Stacy used to date," Lindsey whispered.

What?

Grace looked to the front of the boat where the woman was still dallying, hunched over her camera equipment, her damp brown hair hiding her face. When Grace had been introduced to her a few hours ago, she'd been struck by the woman's brusque demeanor, but she'd seemed competent enough. Until she'd left them and missed the encounter with the tigers altogether.

"Alec and that grumpy woman?" Grace said, skeptical. "Are you sure?"

"Yes. Tyler remembers her, and for what it's worth, he never liked her."

"How long did they date?"

"Tyler thinks it was about a year," Lindsey said.

Oh, right. Stacy. Now Grace remembered. She and Alec had had a few short conversations about exes, and he had mentioned her.

"What are the odds ...." Grace murmured to herself. But then again, Alec had been forced to live on a boat with Grace and her ex, Brad, for three weeks, so Grace really couldn't complain.

She peeked at Stacy again. She wasn't that bad looking, and Grace could grudgingly see why Alec might be attracted to her.

"Did they speak to each other?" Grace asked.

"A little," Lindsey said, "but mostly Alec was pissed that you were in the water getting attacked by sharks. He very quickly put on his tank and jumped in."

ONCE ALEC HAD GOTTEN Grace back to his parents' house, dinner had ensued, and she hadn't seemed inclined to talk about her dive. Even worse, she hadn't said one word about Stacy. Alec knew that Lindsey, or Tyler, would've told her who the woman was to him, so why hadn't Grace grilled him?

That they weren't talking was throwing a wrench into his plan for Christmas Eve.

Grace was scheduled to go back out the next morning and dive again so Craig could get his footage, and Stacy had better be prepared. Still, Alec would bring what equipment he had with him just in case.

Finally, after two games of charades with the entire family, Alec had her alone in their bedroom. He sat on the bed propped up by a few pillows while she was in the bathroom washing her face and brushing her teeth.

His cell phone buzzed on the nightstand. He didn't recognize the number and thought about ignoring it, but at the last second answered.

"Alec Galloway."

"Hi Alec." It was Stacy. "I hope it's okay that I called."

"How did you get my number?"

"Your girlfriend wrote it on the release contract Craig had her sign. You know, in case something happened, and we had to contact someone. You were her someone."

The thought of Grace being that hurt, or worse, didn't improve his mood.

"I guess I should've looked at the paperwork more closely," Stacy continued, "then I would've known you were here."

Grace came out of the bathroom in a long-sleeved T-shirt she'd picked up at a local souvenir stand and sleep shorts. The last few nights she'd slept in a tank top—at least when she wasn't naked beneath him—and he wondered how bad her arms looked if she felt the need to cover them.

The look she gave him as she grabbed a tube of lotion told him she knew exactly who was on the phone, but she busied herself with vigorously slathering her legs.

Time to nip this in the bud. He put his phone on speaker.

"What do you want, Stacy?" he said.

"Do you know Doug Henderson?"

"Yeah, sure," Alec replied. Henderson ran a large underwater filmmaking outfit that had subcontracted Alec and his partner, Double D, a few times.

"Have you worked with him?"

Alec suspected that Stacy already knew he had, and his disappointment surprised him. She was still the same. She didn't really want to catch up for old times' sake, not that he wanted that either, but it chafed that she was still fishing for help with work.

"I have," Alec answered reluctantly.

"He's got a project happening next spring in the Maldives and I've been trying to get my resume in front of him but having no luck. I wondered if you might be able to smooth the way."

Grace glanced at Alec, managing to convey sarcasm and irritation at the same time. How did women do that?

"I don't know," he replied. "It's been a while since I've spoken to Doug."

"Just thought I'd ask. I could email my resume to you if that would help."

Alec took a deep breath. "Let me think about it."

"Sure. I'll see you tomorrow? You're coming out on the boat with Grace, right?"

"Yes."

"Great. I'll see you then."

Alec ended the call.

Grace sat on the edge of the bed, her back to him. "So, you and Stacy," she said. "What's it like seeing her?"

"I'd like to point out that I'm only seeing her because of *you*."

She shrugged and peered at him over her shoulder. "True."

He sighed. "Do you really need to get in the water again tomorrow?"

She shifted to face him. "I'm fine."

He took her hand and pushed up the sleeve. The black and blue welts were becoming more pronounced. "That doesn't look fine to me."

"You, of anyone, know those sharks aren't trying to eat me. And I'm happy to help Craig with his project. Will you come and film it tomorrow?"

"I don't think Stacy would like that."

She pressed her lips together. "I don't like talking shit about anyone, but she really dropped the ball today. If she hadn't, I wouldn't be getting back in the water tomorrow. And tomorrow is Christmas Eve. I'd really like this not to spill over into Christmas, since this is the first holiday we're spending with your parents." She leaned forward and gave him a kiss.

"I don't have all my gear here," he said. "But I can bring my Canon."

"Is that a metaphor?" She kissed him again.

"Don't start anything you're not prepared to finish," he muttered against her lips.

She grinned. "I'm prepared."

He hit the light switch by the bed and let Grace seduce him.

GRACE AWOKE EARLY. She winced from the bruises on her arms, having grown fiercer and more colorful during the night, but it wasn't anything she couldn't endure.

She ran her fingers through Alec's short hair. "Wake up, sleepyhead."

It was four a.m.

Alec reached for her, and she enjoyed the warmth of his bare chest. "Let's stay in bed," he mumbled, his eyes still closed.

It had merit, her body still humming from last night. She hoped no one else in the house had heard them. Normally, she wasn't so randy while in the presence of Alec's parents, as well as Ty and Lindsey, and Brynn and Tristan. But damn, she wanted to erase any memory of Stacy from Alec's head.

Not that Grace was worried about him succumbing to the woman's charms, but it didn't hurt to remind him what he had here. With her.

He finally rose from bed and they both quietly dressed—him in shorts and a hooded blue sweatshirt and she in lightweight black jogging pants and a pink and blue rash guard. She threw on a windbreaker for the early morning chill.

Alec went to the kitchen while she applied a reef-safe sunscreen to her face and secured her blonde hair in a braid.

When she left their bedroom on the second floor and followed the aroma of coffee brewing to the main floor, she was surprised to see Alec's father sitting at the breakfast bar, his laptop open before him.

"Good morning, Jim," she said.

"Morning, Gracie."

"I thought you might need this," Alec said, handing her a mug of coffee.

Normally she wouldn't drink caffeine before getting in the water, but she was grateful for Alec's thoughtfulness. She wasn't freediving, and the dive would be stressful, so the kick from the caffeine was welcome to clear the cobwebs from her head.

"You're up early," Grace said to Jim.

"Couldn't sleep. Thought I might as well get some work done."

"But it's Christmas Eve," she said.

"And why are you up, Grace?" Jim arched a brow. "Headed out for a day of fun?"

She smiled at the tone of his voice. "All right, you've caught me. It's hard to say no to interesting projects."

He smiled. "Here, here." Alec's mom, Lily, said often enough that her husband didn't do well with idle time.

"When will you two be back?" Jim asked as Alec threw a few energy bars, an apple, and two bananas into a soft-sided lunch box.

"If all goes well," Alec said, "before my lazy siblings are up and having their breakfast bagel. No one will even know we were gone."

"Famous last words," Jim said. "Be careful you two."

"We will." Grace planted a kiss on Jim's cheek as they left.

She followed Alec out the front door and climbed into the passenger side of the truck sitting in the driveway.

Alec started the vehicle. "You're such a kiss up to my dad."

"You're just jealous because he likes me more," she teased, holding her coffee mug up so it didn't slosh as Alec backed the truck to the street.

"You can wrangle sharks, so I'm not surprised that you've been able to win over my dad. He's as ornery as any of those tigers you're trying to attract."

She laughed. "True. Maybe that's why he and I get along so well."

ALEC WAS SUITED up and ready to get in the water. Stacy was beside him, having been mostly quiet for the boat ride beyond a cursory greeting when they'd all met at the dock.

At the back of the boat, Craig and Joel were getting Grace into the metal suit.

"You don't have to bring that," Stacy said, her gaze dropping to the camera and the waterproof housing sitting on his lap.

"Grace asked me to."

"Is it serious between you two?" The shadowed look in Stacy's eyes confused Alec. She had left *him*.

"It is."

"I'm happy for you."

"Thanks. And you? How are you?"

"Well, I certainly would like to be anywhere but here," she said, pulling on black neoprene gloves.

Again, Alec was confused. Was it because of him?

"You all didn't have to reach out to Grace," he said, balancing his air tank between his legs.

"What? Oh no. That's not why. In fact, it's been nice to see you again. I just feel like this job is beneath my abilities. It's nothing more than a hack Shark Week stunt."

And there she was, the Stacy he remembered, still a snob when it came to a job she felt was beneath her.

"I wanted to assure you," she continued, "that this isn't reflective of the work I'm capable of. I'd be grateful for your help in reaching out to Doug Henderson."

The slippery, used feeling that had permeated the end of their relationship surfaced, and it was all Alec could do to not shake his head in disappointment. But another concern pressed on him, something far more important than his and Stacy's doomed relationship or her desperation for an "important" job.

Grace's safety depended on the focus of everyone present on this crew. And Stacy's obvious distaste for the assignment showcased her lack thereof.

"Maybe you should stay on the boat," he said to her. "I don't think you have the heart for this."

"You know this work doesn't have anything to do with heart."

Alec stood and shouldered his tank. "You're wrong. It has everything to do with it."

GRACE SAT TUCKED between Lindsey and Brynn on the plush couch in Jim and Lily's home, showing off the bruises on both arms. The guys were on the back porch smoking a traditional Christmas Eve cigar, or so Alec had told her.

"Tell me honestly," Brynn said to Grace. "Weren't you at least a little bit afraid when the tiger shark clamped down?"

"You forget, Brynn," Lindsey said. "Grace had to jam her arm into the beast's mouth. Could you do that if you were afraid?"

"I couldn't do it at all," Brynn declared.

Lily entered the living room carrying a tray, wearing a tasteful red Christmas sweater and her dark hair in a festive curly bob.

Grace took one of the cocktails Lily offered. "I wasn't worried," Grace said. "The chain mail metal suit was solid." Well, maybe she'd been a little worried, but no reason to dwell on that now. The project was over, with Alec grabbing the footage that Craig had needed. Now she could return to vacationing with her boyfriend.

Grace took a sip of the fruity concoction. "It's delicious. Thank you, Lily. Are you sure we can't help in the kitchen?"

Lily set the tray on the coffee table. "No, no. I've got it under control. I'm happy to do it. I want to thank you all for spending the holidays with us. It's not easy getting everyone under one roof, and my boys wouldn't be here without you both." Her gaze encompassed Grace and Lindsey. "Please let your mothers know I appreciate them letting you come."

Both Grace and Lindsey had lost their fathers. Luckily Grace's mother had her sister Chloe, although Chloe was about to leave for work on a sperm whale project on the island of Dominica in the Caribbean. But Lindsey's mother had no one, having lost her husband years ago and more recently Lindsey's sister, both in mountain climbing accidents.

"I'll tell her," Grace said. Then she asked Lindsey, "What's your mother doing for Christmas?"

"Believe it or not, she's on a cruise with another widow she's been friends with for a while. I think she was happy to skip all the Christmas hoopla and just relax."

"Because next year you and Ty might have a little one running around?" Brynn asked.

Lindsey's face went red, and she laughed nervously.

"Don't tease me, Brynn. I'm so ready for grandchildren." Lily pinned a hopeful gaze on all three of them in turn, and Grace felt like they were in a line up.

"Mom …." The alarm in Brynn's voice was interrupted when the back door slid open, and the men all filed in.

Lily stood. "It's time for Secret Santa, so sit down."

They had randomly chosen names a month ago, and now the gifts all sat on a side table beside the Christmas tree that occupied the corner of the living room, decorated in colored lights, seashells, and ornaments ranging from turtles to dolphins to hammerhead sharks. Grace loved it and had sat in one of the cozy chairs with a cup of hot chocolate more than once since she and Alec had arrived. That she'd imagined a child or two—Alec's children—running around one day, she'd kept to herself. Although she wondered if Lily had some sort of psychic power and had known that Grace's biological clock had started ticking in an annoying way that was becoming harder to ignore.

"Anyone want a beer?" Tyler asked.

"I've made drinks," Lily said, waving at him to sit down.

His brows knit together. "Those seem a bit … fruity looking."

"It's just cranberry juice and a bit of gin." She forced one into his hand.

Tyler balanced the drink as he wedged himself against Lindsey, forcing Grace to lean into Brynn, so Brynn left to perch on the arm of the single chair that Tristan had sunk into. Grace tried to get Alec's attention, to get him to sit beside her, but he was standing near the kitchen, avoiding her gaze. He rubbed at his neck, as if he were nervous, pacing a bit.

For a split second, Stacy Finnegan loomed large. Was that why he was anxious? Had something happened? Was he contemplating how to let Grace down easy?

No. No way. But her palms broke into a sweat. She grabbed one of Lily's cocktails and drank the entire thing.

"Okay," Lily said, searching the gifts. "First up we have Jim." She handed her husband his present.

"It's from Tyler," Jim said and unwrapped the large rectangular box. A bottle of scotch.

Brynn frowned. "I thought we had a twenty-dollar limit."

"And you believed that?" Tyler rebutted.

"Thank you, Ty," Jim said. "We'll break it out after dinner."

Lily grabbed another gift, a large gift bag. "For Lindsey from Grace."

Lindsey removed the tissue paper and pulled out diving equipment—a mask, snorkel, and flippers.

"Thank you," Lindsey said, "but I'm not going shark diving with you."

"That's okay," Grace replied. "How about some turtles?"

"Do they bite?"

"Well …." Grace didn't want to lie. "Sometimes."

"I'll try these out in the pool."

"This one is for me from Tristan," Lily said. She opened the small box, revealing a silver armband.

"It's a replica," Tristan said, resting a hand on Brynn's knee, "from one of the richest collections of Viking-age objects ever found in the United Kingdom, discovered in Galloway, Scotland, around 900 A.D."

"What an exquisite and thoughtful gift," Lily said, admiring it. "Thank you."

"Oh for the love of God, did no one follow the rules of this exchange?" Brynn exclaimed. "That couldn't possibly have cost twenty dollars." She stared down at Tristan from her perch. "You could've told me."

"It's your mother, Brynn. I'm no fool. I want to date her daughter. I'm not giving her soap."

Brynn crossed her arms in defeat, and Tristan laughed, squeezing her knee.

"This is from me to Tyler," Lily said.

It was a framed photo of his chocolate lab, Meryl Streep, or otherwise known as Muck.

Ty grinned. "It's beautiful, Mom. Thanks."

"Well, she and Grace are my only grandchildren at the moment," Lily said, referring to Alec's golden lab whom he had named Grace Kelly.

Alec had begun referring to the Graces in his life as Grace One and Grace Two, although Grace was never certain which one she was.

A silence ensued. That was the second comment from Lily about grandchildren in an hour, and Grace pretended not to notice, instead focusing on smoothing out invisible wrinkles on her black pants.

"This is for you, Brynn." Her mother handed her an envelope. "It's from your father."

Brynn opened it, revealing two plane tickets. "Tahiti?" She raised her eyes to her father, confusion in her gaze.

"Take a vacation. And take Magee along."

Grace knew through Alec that Jim had been annoyed when Brynn had quit her graduate program in archaeology shortly after she'd met Tristan, and instead had gone to work for Tristan's cousin, Shea Hartigan, at Hartigan Archaeology and Consulting. So this gesture was nothing short of huge.

"I can't accept this, Dad. It's way over the twenty-dollar limit," she added, in a quiet voice.

"Take it. Both of you. With my blessing." And with that, Jim was done talking about it.

Brynn, however, pushed off the couch and gave her father a big hug.

Lily handed a gift to Tristan. "From Lindsey." It was a sweatshirt with the slogan: *Physics – Why shit does stuff.*

"Since you're Mr. Physics himself," Lindsey said to him.

"Thank you."

Lily handed a small gift to Alec. Brynn lunged for it, trying to snatch it away. "Let me get something different," she said.

Alec held it away from her. "No. That's not how this works."

He tore open the paper, revealing a small stuffed animal that seemed to resemble a great white shark.

Tyler laughed. "Did you steal that from a child?"

Brynn planted her hands on her hips. "No, of course not."

"How much did you spend?" Ty continued to goad her. "Three dollars?"

"Six seventy-five, if you must know," she ground out. "And I would like to point out that I was the *only* one who abided by the rules, except for maybe mom with Tyler's dog photo."

"I'll confess that I spent forty-five on the frame," Lily admitted, looking sheepish.

"Brynn, I love it," Alec said, tossing it playfully to Grace.

She caught it and felt better about his mood from the gleam in his gaze.

Brynn went back to resting on Tristan's chair and he folded her into his embrace, pulling her onto his lap. "Merry Christmas, cheapskate."

Brynn laughed.

"Wait a minute," Lily was saying. "There's no more gifts but Grace doesn't have one. And you can't regift the shark, Alec."

Alec had gone still, and everyone shifted their attention to him.

"Are you my Secret Santa?" Grace asked him.

"I am."

"This is sounding rigged to me," Brynn murmured. "He's the one who organized who got who this year."

He pulled a jewelry box from his pocket, and Grace's heart stopped.

Oh my God.

Someone gasped and Grace was pretty sure it was Brynn.

Alec went down on one knee and opened the case, revealing a sparkling diamond ring.

"Grace Elizabeth Mann, will you marry me?"

Grace was stunned. She'd had no idea. None at all. She and Alec had only recently moved in together, and while it was going well, she never wanted to overplay her hand by expecting anything more.

With all eyes on her, she swallowed nervously.

"Are you sure?" she whispered.

"Absolutely sure." Alec's blue eyes were focused solely on her.

"Then yes, absolutely yes."

He removed the ring from the jewelry box and slid it onto the third finger of her left hand. She wrapped her arms around him and kissed him, hard. Everyone cheered, and soon Grace was being hugged by one after another.

Laughing and crying a bit too, she took it all in, her heart feeling full. Through it all she couldn't take her eyes off Alec, who watched her with such open affection that she felt as if she were in a dream. He was wild and fierce, honest and caring, and nothing had ever felt more right in her life.

If there was only one sadness in her heart, it was knowing her father wasn't here to be a part of it.

Oh Daddy, I wish you could have known him.

ALEC ENTERED THEIR BEDROOM. It was late on Christmas Eve, and Grace had just gotten off the phone talking to her mother.

"How's Susie?" Alec asked, dropping on the bed beside her, smelling of the celebratory cigar he'd shared with his dad, Tyler, and Tristan while Grace and the girls had decorated Christmas cookies and drunk eggnog laced with a bit of the scotch Ty had given Jim. Then she'd excused herself to call her mom.

"She's good," Grace said, rolling to her side to face him. "The ring is so beautiful, Alec." The platinum band had tiny diamonds embedded along it with the main diamond atop. It was elegant and understated.

"I'm glad you like it," he said. "The platinum won't tarnish if it gets wet. I thought it suited you."

"It does. Did your mother help you pick it out?"

"No. I sweated this one out all on my own."

Grace kissed him. "I love it. And I love you. My mom's very happy for us, but I think she must've been talking to your mom."

"How's that? I didn't tell anyone I was going to propose, not even Double D."

"She referenced grandchildren at least three times, and your mom mentioned them earlier this evening. That's a lot of Grandma Jedi mind tricks. I'm not sure we'll survive the onslaught."

He brought a hand to her hip and scooted closer, his face mere inches from hers.

"I'm not opposed to babies, Grace."

She grinned. "Let's worry about the wedding first."

"Okay, let's have it. I'm sure you girls had plenty of ideas while making cookies."

"Some," she said. "Your mom thought Telluride would be nice, and Lindsey agreed, having just been there. Brynn thinks we ought to go aquatic."

"What do you want?" he asked.

"Well, those tickets your dad gave Brynn got me thinking. Tahiti in August has humpbacks."

"And sharks."

"Oceanic white tips," she said against his lips.

"Have you been looking at my work schedule?"

"No. Why?"

"I've been offered to film the Pro Tahiti Surf Championship in Teahupo'o in late August."

"Are you going to take it?" she asked.

"Well, I only just learned about it, and I wasn't sure I'd accept because it depended on your schedule."

"I think maybe a wedding is on my schedule," she said, rolling on top of him.

He ran his hands along her backside, tugging on the tank top she wore. Alec no longer seemed phased by the purple welts on her arms, so she wasn't going to bother hiding them.

"Then I'll think about taking it," he said.

She braced herself above him. "You know, you seemed a bit anxious while we were doing the gift exchange, and for a moment I worried it might be about Stacy."

"Seriously? Brynn was right when she said I rigged the Secret Santa. I've been planning this for weeks."

Grace didn't think it was possible to feel even more warm and fuzzy inside, but she did. As cozy as the Christmas socks on her feet, a gift from her sister, Chloe, when she, Grace, and their mother had celebrated the holiday early a week ago.

"Weeks?" she said. "We only moved in together two months ago."

"Stacy was never a problem," he added. "If anything, seeing her made me realize how lucky I am to have found you. She lacks the one thing you have in abundance."

"Sharks on the brain?"

He chuckled. "No. Heart. I think that, more than anything, was why it was never going to work with her. But I should tell you that I'm going to give her that referral. I'll let Doug decide if he wants to hire her. She's not a bad filmmaker."

"But you're better."

"Damn straight. Did you talk to Chloe?"

"No," Grace answered. "She's on a flight to Dominica as we speak. I'll call her in the morning."

"Why is she flying on Christmas Eve?"

"My mom said something about her school advisor having a family emergency, and Chloe needing to take over the sperm whale project. She was in a bit of a panic and decided to head out a few days early. Tickets are a lot cheaper on Christmas Eve."

"Is your mom okay on her own?" he asked.

"Are you kidding? She's got Grace Kelly and Meryl Streep to keep her company," she said, referring to Alec and Tyler's Labradors. Her mom had graciously offered to watch them so they didn't have to go into a kennel since all the Galloways would be in Hawai'i. "She's practicing for those grandbabies."

"Then I guess we'd better get started."

Thank you so much for reading. Your support means the world to me. As always, reviews are much appreciated!
~ Kristy xx

Sign up for my newsletter to stay updated on all my book news. Visit kmccaffrey.com/subscribe/ to join.

The Pathway Series

Romance, danger, and high adventure guaranteed!

DEEP BLUE

Biologist and free diver Dr. Grace Mann teams up with filmmaker Alec Galloway to make a documentary about great white sharks. But as their chemistry catches fire, deadly dangers lurk below the surface ...

COLD HORIZON

Two years ago, Lindsey Coulson lost her sister on K2, the second highest mountain on earth. Searching for answers, she sets out to climb the Savage Mountain, but to get there, she'll need handsome, enigmatic Tyler Galloway.

ANCIENT WINDS

Archaeologist Brynn Galloway partners with sexy mercenary physicist Dr. Tristan Magee to track down a rare Sumerian artifact, but in the Bolivian jungle there are no barriers ... least of all between them.

A PATHWAY SHORT ADVENTURE COLLECTION

(Three short stories)

Deep Blue Australia

Dr. Grace Mann and Alec Galloway travel to Western Australia for a commercial shoot with great white sharks.

Deep Blue Réunion Island

Grace joins Alec on a trip to the French island of Réunion to document efforts in relocating aggressive bull sharks from the coastline.

Deep Blue Cocos Island

Alec is hired to film Grace and several distinguished female marine scientists in the waters off Cocos Island.

COLD HORIZON: Telluride

(A short story)

After surviving a harrowing descent of K2, Lindsey Coulson has serious doubts about continuing her life of a high-altitude mountain climber. Ty Galloway has settled into a nine-to-five routine with his new job as editor-in-chief of Mountaineer Magazine, but the monotony is already beginning to chafe. A weekend away in Telluride, Colorado, might just open new doors of possibility for the couple.

SHARK REEF

(A short story)

Dr. Gabe O'Grady has had it bad for Jen Fairfield since they met, but their timing has always been off. When he learns she's about to spend three weeks tagging great white sharks with a notoriously sketchy filmmaker, Gabe inserts himself into the project to protect her. But her indifference confounds him. As he tries to rekindle the friendship she seems determined to walk away from, he must also keep her safe from one of the most dangerous predators on earth.

SAPPHIRE WAVES

(A Novella)

Missy fell for Josh when they were interns at Shark Lab in the

Bahamas, but a family tragedy cut short their romance. Four years later they're both on the same diving team to study a blue hole. And the feelings are still there ...

(Includes a bonus story, *Deep Blue Hawai'i* - Dr. Grace Mann and her boyfriend, underwater filmmaker Alec Galloway, are in the Aloha State for a Galloway family Christmas. While surfing Pipe is on the agenda for the boys, Grace finds a way to get in the water with tiger sharks, but can Alec convince her to stay on dry land long enough for an important question?)

Learn more at kmccaffrey.com/pathway-book-page/

ABOUT THE AUTHOR

Kristy McCaffrey has been writing since she was very young, but it wasn't until she was a stay-at-home mom that she considered becoming published. A fascination with science led her to earn two mechanical engineering degrees—she did her undergraduate work at Arizona State University and her graduate studies at the University of Pittsburgh—but storytelling has always been her passion. She writes both contemporary adventures and award-winning historical western romances.

An Arizona native, Kristy and her husband reside in the desert where they frequently remove (rescue) rattlesnakes from their property, go for runs among the cactus, and plan trips to far-off places like the Orkney Islands or Machu Picchu. But mostly, she works 12-hour days and enjoys at-home date nights with her sweetheart, which usually include Will Ferrell movies and sci-fi flicks. Her four children have all flown the nest, so she lavishes her maternal instincts on Jeb, an American Bulldog her family rescued in 2021. He has his own Instagram account at @jeb_therescue.

Connect with Kristy

Website: kmccaffrey.com
Newsletter: kmccaffrey.com/subscribe
Facebook: facebook.com/AuthorKristyMcCaffrey
Instagram: instagram.com/kristymccaffreybooks/
BookBub: bookbub.com/authors/kristy-mccaffrey
TikTok: tiktok.com/@kristymccaffrey

www.ingramcontent.com/pod-product-compliance
Lightning Source LLC
Chambersburg PA
CBHW072240190626
46809CB00018B/2857

* 9 7 8 1 9 5 2 8 0 1 3 8 9 *